GW00480716

ISBN: 9798394898822

Imprint: Independently published

a Scottie RAMONE COZY MYSTERY

BETTER OFF
Shortbread

LONDON LOVETT

one

. . .

"SCOTTIE, you're as giddy as a Chihuahua," I muttered to myself as I stood in the half-finished kitchen of my future bakery. It was a phrase my grandmother, Nana, used to say when I was younger and overly excited about an upcoming event like a sleepover with friends or Christmas morning. She'd grown up with a tiny Chihuahua named Ollie who would get so excited about a walk or a treat he'd tremble until he tinkled. Fortunately, I'd always managed to avoid the embarrassment of a tinkle, but as a child I did occasionally get so excited and nervous I'd throw up, like on the way to school for my solar system presentation in third grade when I tossed my breakfast in Nana's car. We had to throw Saturn away, leaving my model a planet short. (Arguably, the best planet with its showy rings). I could easily sympathize with Ollie.

"Scottie, we're going to have to move the work table two

inches to the right to bring the kitchen up to code on oven clearance," Cody's remark pulled me from my thoughts.

"Not a problem," I said.

Cody, my general contractor, was a sturdily-built forty-something man with greasy hair and an impressive tattoo of a German Shepherd on the back of his forearm. Brutus had been his best friend growing up. I'd heard more than one tale, possibly true, possibly embellished, about how Brutus had saved Cody from harm. There was even a story where Cody had fallen into an abandoned mine shaft, and Brutus ran three miles home to summon help. It was hard to know if Cody had grown up watching too many *Lassie* reruns or if he'd actually had so many misadventures in his youth, he required constant heroism from his amazing dog. Either way, it wasn't for me to question. In fact, true or not, I found the harrowing, happy-ending stories charming. Besides, it was hard not to like a guy with a tattoo of his beloved dog on his arm.

I'd interviewed a parade of contractors, including one that my friend and the town ranger, Dalton Braddock, had recommended. No one could start the job until after winter. That just wasn't going to work. After wasting a month feeling majorly sorry for myself, I was ready to start my dream business of a vintage bakery. I worried (and Nana did as well, though she never said it aloud) that if I had to spend a long, dreary winter with nothing to push me out of bed in the morning, I would fall back into the doldrums that had overtaken me after I left my fiancé, my job and all the trappings of city life.

I found Cody's contractor ad on the back of one of those free penny saving mailers that usually went straight from mailbox to recycling bin. If I was being honest, I didn't just randomly find the ad. Nana had opened the mailer to the page with Cody's phone number and quotes from several glowing reviews. She left it folded neatly next to my plate of pancakes. I laughed at first reminding her that the penny-saving mailers were more for things like a free second-hand stove or a local chicken farmer's eggs than for a contractor, but she insisted I was being a snob. Which, in retrospect, I was. I called Cody. He'd had a cancellation in his schedule and was available. He was confident and timely and came with good references. I hired him on the spot. It was my first good business decision in what I hoped would be a long parade of good decisions. Cody and his no-nonsense, hard-working team had made a lot of progress. I could see my kitchen taking shape. It was no longer impossible to imagine myself standing in the middle of my bustling bakery surrounded by delicious scents and smiling customer faces. My dream was slowly coming together and I was, for lack of a better word, giddy. Was there really a better word than giddy? It was such a fun, expressive word that it, in my opin-ion, should have been used more often.

"Cody, I'm heading out. Call me if you need anything, and thanks for all the hard work. This place is really coming together." The cabinets for the ovens and the proofers had been installed, and all of the electrical and plumbing, at least the rough stuff, had been completed and signed off by inspec-tors. It wouldn't be long before my equipment arrived. Cody and I planned it so that the kitchen would be ready first. While they worked on the front of the shop, I could test recipes and figure out a good workflow. It would be a lot of hard work, but I knew from experience once a schedule was formed and I got into the rhythm of creating daily pastries, breads and cakes, the bakery would run smoothly.

"See you later, Scottie," Cody called as I headed out.

Early fall had enveloped Ripple Creek with its dry breezes, crisp temperatures and glorious explosion of autumn colors. In between the smoky blues and forest greens of the junipers, pines and fir trees, the fiery gold and orange of the region's quaking aspens stood out like blazing torches. The town was beautiful and lush in spring and summer, but there was always something about fall that reminded you that you were living in a piece of paradise. In the distance, the familiar boisterous, in-flight conversation of Canadian geese echoed over the valley as a long V of them returned to their favorite fall and winter grounds. Critters that had scurried through trees and over forest floors in summer would soon quiet down, readying themselves for a long, harsh winter, but you could always count on the geese to remind you that nature up in these mountains was abundant and wonderful.

Fall was so spectacular in the Rockies, we could always count on a steady stream of visitors and tourists rolling through town. A silver van with the words Nature Quest Photography Club written on the side in black lettering was parked in front of the general store. Nana's best friend, Roxi, ran the place. Her freshly made sandwiches and salads were a big draw for visitors.

I needed another bag of sugar from Roxi's store. I still hadn't set up my own purchase orders from a wholesale vendor mostly because I had no place to store bulk items. Cody's team was working on the stockroom and a space for the massive refrigerator I was going to need for the bakery. In the meantime, I was clearing the baking shelves in Roxi's store. She didn't mind too much, but I knew that once the calendar flipped to November and visions of holiday baking floated through the air, she'd need her shelves stocked. Cody said we were on schedule for the stockroom to be ready in two weeks. So far, he hadn't let me down.

Roxi was busy checking a few people out at the register. She waved briefly before putting several sandwiches and drinks into a paper bag. The photography group was easy to recognize in their pristine outdoor gear, puffy coats, neatly rolled beanies and hardly used hiking boots. It seemed the club was comprised of three men and two women. One of the men seemed to be giving out orders on the best snacks and drinks for their adventure. He had a somewhat arrogant tone that immediately made me bristle. His khaki pants were pleated down the front, and his black beanie sat roundly on his head. He was short and lean in stature with ramrod straight posture and a commanding presence for someone his size.

"Shayla," he said sharply as he picked up a bag of trail mix. "You've got to put down those crackers." He laughed and it was an irritating sound. "I said something with nutritional value." He sounded more like a parent than a co-club member. Shayla, a woman of medium height with brown hair and a fringe of bangs sticking out below the rim of her bright blue beanie, was properly chastised. She blushed with embarrassment as she quietly put the crackers back on the shelf.

I headed to my usual hangout, the baking aisle. I'd decided to make some delicious and buttery shortbread. The weekly farmer's market had ended along with the last remnants of summer. As soon as the leaves turned yellow, local artists and produce growers rolled up their banners, dismantled their kiosks and packed everything up for the next year. I'd done the same. After a successful season at the market, it was time for a new venue to give people a sample of my treats. I'd toyed with the idea of setting up my own little sidewalk sale right in front of my soon-to-be bakery. My plans weren't solid yet, but I thought shortbread was a nice, easy treat to sell from a sidewalk table.

The arrogant photographer (the name I'd given him) clipped in front of me in line for the register. He was rather rude about it, and it didn't escape Roxi's notice. She scowled at him from behind her checkout stand. With a five-pound bag of sugar under each arm, I shrugged to let her know it was fine.

"Chaz," the other woman with the group called as she approached him in line. She held up a bottle of sparkling water. "I'm going to need more than plain water." The woman had cinnamon brown hair plaited down her back in a long braid. She had bright green eyes and was dressed in the height of outdoor fashion with slick black leggings tucked into fur-topped boots. She wore an emerald green puffy vest over a black turtleneck, and somewhere in the midst of pulling on her stylish and not the least bit rugged attire, she'd doused herself with copious amounts of perfume. It wasn't a bad scent. It just would have been better in a lighter concentration.

Chaz didn't look convinced about her need for sparkling water. "Fiona, our water is literally the same substance only without the bubbles. These sparkling water companies sure know how to dupe people out of hard-earned money."

Fiona ignored his comment and placed the bottle on the counter along with his trail snacks.

Shayla, the woman who'd been lectured about nutritious snacks, stood behind me in line clutching a bag of trail mix. The other group members, two men with less pristine outerwear and cameras hanging around their necks, I supposed in case a moose or elk decided to enter the market, stood behind Shayla. They were having a conversation about the types of birds they hoped to see on their hike. After the flurry of bird activity in the spring and summer, the skies and trees in the Rockies tended to grow quiet. Some species had already migrated, and others, now finished with the nesting period, had flown off to wait for the long winter to rear its frosty head. Naturally, bald eagles came up in their conversation. We had several in the area, but they were elusive to say the least. A hiker in town for a few days would have just as much luck spotting Bigfoot.

Chaz, a name that fit the man perfectly, paid for his snacks and told everyone to hurry so they could get to the campsite and set up tents. He strolled out, and Fiona smiled at everyone before following closely at his heels.

Roxi rolled her eyes. "I guess it takes all kinds," she muttered. "And speaking of all kinds, what is our wonderful town baker up to? Seems like things are moving along across the street."

I sighed to show her how exhausting it all was. "They're moving along. It doesn't help that we've got Jack Frost nipping at our heels. I just hope he doesn't come early. Remember that year when it snowed in September? Fall was obliterated before we even had a chance to pick pumpkins."

"I remember it well," Roxi said. "It killed off our autumn tourist season. What are you baking this time?" she asked as I set down the sugar to pull out my debit card.

"Shortbread. I'm just trying to decide the best way to sell it now that the farmer's market has shut down."

Roxi put her hands on her hips, almost as if angry about what I'd said. "Wouldn't it be cool if you had, oh, I don't know, a close friend who also happened to own a small market where things such as shortbread could be sold?"

I blinked at her a second trying to separate the sarcasm from the real stuff. I squinted one eye. "Was that your long, Nana-style way of telling me I could sell my baked goods here, in your store?"

"Yes, silly. We could make a place right up front at the cash register. That way, after people have picked their sandwiches, they can finish their lunch purchase off with one of your treats. I have a few empty display cases in the stockroom. We could set up a cute little bakery cart, and you could fill it with whatever you bake for the week."

There was some of that giddiness again. "Roxi, that would

be wonderful. Thank you so much. Naturally, we'll share the profits."

"I think fifteen percent is fair." Roxi was a good friend. She was a great deal younger than Nana, but they'd hit it off almost instantly because they were both independent, strong-willed and confident. Roxi was also a clever businesswoman. For a long time, at least until Roxi took hold of the reins, the Ripple Creek Market was a dingy little store stocked with cookie packages that were far past their expiration date, trail mix that was as stale as an Egyptian mummy and sodas that had lost their fizz. She bought the place and turned it almost instantly into the fresh, buzzing-with-activity centerpiece of the town. Her handmade sandwiches really helped put her store and our town on the map. Having my goodies at her store was a dream come true.

"Fifteen is perfect. I'll start working on the shortbread today. I just need to perfect my recipe to arrive at the right texture—softly crunchy, and the right flavor—buttery with a sweet edge." I picked up the sugar. "Thanks again, Roxi. I'll see you later."

I left the store feeling even more energetic about my short-bread endeavor.

two

· · ·

ESME ADAMS, my newest Ripple Creek buddy and soon-to-be business neighbor (once the bakery opened) had stepped out to check the book display in her front window. I was so excited about selling my baked goods in Roxi's store, I hurried across the street to tell her.

"Guess who'll be selling baked goods in Roxi's market?" I asked as I crossed over to the bookstore.

Esme hadn't seen me and spun around with a smile. "Scottie, nice to see you. Wait, let me guess. Baked goods? I've heard there's a very talented baker in town, and she'll soon be delighting the locals with her flaky pastries and gooey cinnamon rolls. I sure hope it's her."

I nodded. "The very same. I was telling Roxi that I didn't know how to sell my goods now that the street fair shut down for the season, and she kindly offered me a display case in her store."

"That sounds like a win-win for everyone." Esme motioned with her head toward her shop. She had only opened the Nine Lives Bookstore a month earlier, and it was already a popular place for locals and visitors alike. Her colorful, thematic displays (this month's being all things spooky and weird to get ready for Halloween) attracted people's attention. Esme had a knack for design. She'd even given me some great ideas for creating a welcoming interior with a nostalgic edge for the front of my bakery.

We stepped into the bookstore. Esme had set up a tea station, complete with an herbal tea of the day for people who wanted to sit in one of her cozy nooks and read. Today's tea was cinnamon apple, and it lent a comforting fragrance to the air. Earl, her massive tabby, plodded out from behind a paperback display to greet us. He purred loudly and rubbed Esme's ankles.

"Too early for lunch, Earl. Go take another nap, and don't worry, you'll be the first to know when the tuna can is opened." As if he understood every word, and knowing cats he most likely did, he trotted off to one of the corner stacks to curl up and nap.

It turned out the shop had a handful of customers. It seemed the photography club had decided to stop in at the local bookstore before starting their adventure. Shayla, the woman with the poor snack choices, came out from the aisle. "Excuse me, do you work here?" she asked Esme.

Esme glanced pointedly down at her dark green apron with the name of the bookstore emblazoned across it before nodding. "Yes, I do. How can I help you?"

"We're looking for a book. It's called *Nature Scapes* by Chaz Voorman. We can't find it. You must have sold out of your copies."

Chaz emerged from the same aisle with a look of concern. "Your shelves are sorely lacking. My book *Nature Scapes* was voted one of the top photography collections in 2010."

"Oh, well that might be why it's not here," Esme said. "There have been a number of new photographic journals published since then. I try to keep up with whatever is new or up-and-coming." It was a shame Esme had to explain herself. It seemed she had immediately registered the same opinion of the man as me. "However, I can order you a copy. It'll take a few weeks. I could mail it to you if you want to leave your name and address."

Chaz's laugh was dry and harsh. "Why would I order my own book? I have ten copies sitting on my bookshelf at home, but you're depriving your customers of a high-quality book by not having it on your shelves. You should order some now." It was more of a command than a suggestion. Esme flicked an annoyed look my way.

"You're right. I'll get you a piece of paper. You can write down the title, author and publisher. I'll add it to next week's purchase order." I couldn't tell if she was serious or merely humoring the man. I suspected it was the latter. Esme walked to her counter to get a piece of paper and pen.

The rest of the group looked slightly embarrassed about their friend's behavior. Rightfully so. Fiona, the water connoisseur, looked angry. She put her hands on her slim hips and turned to him. "Chaz, you didn't have to be so rude about it. Not every store is going to carry your book. After all, it's a decade old. The publisher might not even have any copies to send."

"Oh, so the silly woman who wastes good money on bubbles, actual air, you know the stuff we breathe for free, is suddenly an expert on publishing."

"I'm leaving." Fiona twirled around on her fur-frosted boots and stomped out of the store. One of the other men, a forty-something, with a thick head of blond hair that was brushed back off his face, followed her out in his beefy looking hiking boots.

"You don't need to follow her, Allen. She's a big girl." Chaz's jaw was clenched tightly. Allen ignored him and pushed angrily out the front door. The second woman, Shayla, the one who dared to consider crackers, stood silently near the tea cart, taking it all in with a good deal of reflection. I could almost read a thought bubble above her head. It said, "why on earth did I join this club?"

Esme thrust the paper and pen at the man. It seemed, like Fiona, Esme had had it too. I was fairly certain there would be no order of Chaz's *wondrous* book of photos. He seemed to gather that too. He rudely handed her back the paper and pen and marched out behind the other two. Shayla nodded politely at Esme and me before walking out in a cloud of embarrassment.

The last remaining photographer was smiling weakly as he returned a book about birding back to the shelf. With his scruffy beard and longish hair, he fit in the least with the group. Instead of the new off-the-rack outdoor gear, he'd opted for wrinkled, faded cargo pants. Each pocket seemed to be filled with something, and they were weighing the pants down low on his hips. His flannel shirt was the kind that had reached that premier level of wonderful softness only a well-worn flannel shirt could achieve.

"Hello, I'm Kevin. You'll have to excuse Chaz. Actually, no, you don't have to excuse him at all," he said with a chuckle. "I hate always having to apologize for that guy. After all, I'm not his parent. I didn't raise him. I just got unlucky in that I joined my local photography club, and that guy came with it. He's the president." Kevin rolled his eyes. "He has six more months in his term and then the rest of us are plotting a coup. Not an actual coup, of course, but we're going to oust him from the White House. He's terrorized the group long enough." He adjusted the camera hanging around his neck as his eyes swept around the store. "Nice place. Great bookstore, and it's only made better by not having Chaz Voorman's book on the shelf." He laughed at his remark. We joined him.

"The sad thing is," Esme started, "I would have gladly ordered it if he'd been a bit more civil about the whole thing. I think it's safe to say, I won't be carrying that book unless someone comes in specifically to order it. Even then, I might try and lead them toward a newer photography book."

"Do you have a published book?" I asked Kevin.

He was surprised by the question. He shook his head once. "No, unfortunately, I don't have the connections like ole' Chaz. He's probably more bluster than talent, but don't tell him I said that. I've got a website—Kevin's Photography. I sell my photos directly through the site. I do well. It's easier than messing with a publisher." He paused. "Sorry, I don't mean to disparage publishers."

Esme laughed. "You don't have to tell me about publishers. I've been working on a book for a long time. Every time I approach a publisher I get rejected before they even open my query."

I looked over at her. "I didn't know you were a writer too."

Esme tucked her black hair behind her ear. "I'm not. According to publishers."

A few customers came in. Esme hurried off to help them.

"Where is the club staying?" I asked. "I heard mention of tents."

Kevin reached into one of his many pockets. It seemed he knew exactly where his inventory was. He pulled out a folded-up brochure that I recognized immediately.

"Ah, you're going up to Blue Jay Ridge," I said.

He unfolded the paper to be sure. "Yep. I take it we'll see blue jays?"

"If there's one bird you can count on up here, it's blue jays."

He rubbed his scraggly beard in thought. "Eagles?"

"Only if you happen to be standing in the right place at the right time and if all the stars are lined up in your favor."

He laughed. "Then I won't take it too personally if I don't see one because the stars rarely line up in my favor." Kevin was the opposite of Chaz in every way. "Guess I better get to the van before a brawl breaks out. Just kidding, of course. Once we get out in nature and all of us enter our own *zone* with our cameras and lenses, things calm down."

"Good luck, and you never know when those stars might line up. Keep a lookout near water. There are a few ponds up there. Eagles love the water."

"Right. Thanks." He left the store.

Esme walked up next to me. "Interesting group. That bully, Chaz, better watch his back. He's the guy we would have pranked in summer camp."

I looked over at her. "A writer and a prankster. I'm learning a whole lot about my new friend."

"There won't be much more. I'm pretty much 'what you see is what you get.' I do, however, like to smear peanut butter on my graham crackers. So, there's that."

We both had a good laugh as I waved and walked out of the bookstore. My phone beeped as I stepped out into the sharp autumn sun. It was a text from Cade, another new friend in Ripple Creek. It seemed I'd chosen a perfect time to move back to my hometown.

"Hey, Ramone, it's been awhile. I've got a new kind of coffee. Hazelnut. Join me for a cup?"

I texted back. "I never turn down an offer of hazelnut coffee. I'll be right over."

three

. . .

CADE RAFFERTY HAD MOVED into his ancestral home on the Gramby Estate earlier this year. The phrase ancestral home might have been too posh of a description. The mansion had fallen into disrepair over the decades, and the once artistically planned gardens were mostly filled with pushy weeds, determined dandelions and out of control shrubs. Cade was a successful author with a wry sense of humor and a carefree attitude that I admired greatly. We'd become fast friends, and I always looked forward to a chat over coffee.

The lush overgrowth of summer was slowly receding, and soon the expansive grounds would turn brown and dormant and altogether less wild. An angry relative had vandalized the three statues the family patriarch and original owner of the estate had commissioned of himself. The heads had been chopped clean off. Having three headless statues in the garden had become disconcerting enough that Cade had the remaining portions of the statues hauled away and demolished.

Cade was wearing a dark gray sweater over a pair of faded jeans. Sunlight glinted off his black sunglasses and his white smile as I climbed up to the top of the garden where the house loomed like a stately old home with a haunted house edge.

"I hope I didn't hype the coffee up too much. The pop of hazelnut is sort of lacking now that I've given it a good taste." He smiled again and handed me a cup with fragrant steam curling up from it.

"It's all in the aroma." I breathed in deeply. "Yep, that's hazelnut." I took a sip. "Not bad. I've had better, but you can't complain when someone hands you a freshly brewed cup of Joe."

We made our way into the house and sat at the round, wooden dining table, a piece of furniture he'd added just a week ago. The kitchen cabinets had been repaired. Cade decided to keep the original oak cabinets after he determined they were the well-built wooden kind that could never be replaced without massive amounts of money. Just having the doors all hang straight on their hinges and close properly had made a world of difference. The faded black and white tile floor was staying as well. I would have kept it too. It lent the whole kitchen a romantic, country feel. Although, I was sure that was not the feel stodgy old Arthur Gramby had been going for when he built the house.

Cade relaxed back against the chair. It creaked like old bones. The dark gray sweater made the green come out in his hazel eyes. More than once I'd asked myself was this a crush, or was it something else? I certainly felt comfortable with Cade, more so than with any other man I'd met, including Jonathan Rathbone, the man I dated and lived with for years. I'd never felt as relaxed or happy with John as I was with Cade. Maybe, I'd finally moved past having crushes and onto something more substantial. Was there a word for an adult crush? Profound admiration—that was a good term for the way I felt about Cade. If only I could get rid of the silly crush I had on Dalton Braddock. Then maybe I could officially consider myself a modern woman and a levelheaded adult. Unfortunately, I still got the occasional weak knees and stomach flutters whenever I had an unexpected run in with my childhood crush. His upcoming nuptials hadn't done enough to dampen those reactions.

Cade took a sip of his coffee, then lowered the cup to the table. He wore a large gold ring on his pinky. No permanent dent from a wedding band. Although, he'd mentioned his ex-wife in passing occasionally. "So, tell me, Ramone, what have you been up to this morning?"

"Oh goodie, I get to talk about me. I'm a big proponent of that."

"Then I'm all ears. But make it good. These ears get easily bored."

"Jeez, no pressure. Just tell a riveting story to a man who literally spends his day writing riveting stories. I do have something fun. Today, I met, or, I should say, stood in the vicinity of a man whose conceit, arrogance, vanity, you name it was off the charts."

Cade sat forward with interest. "He sounds awful. Go on," he prodded.

My posture deflated some when I realized I didn't have much else to go with my assessment of Mr. Chaz Voorman. "Right. Well. First of all, he apparently considered himself the supreme commander of all things snack related."

Cade squinted one eye. He had enviably long, dark lashes. "Snack related?"

"Yes, he was telling his friends what kinds of snacks they should take on their hike. He's a big fan of trail mix. He also considers sparkling water a scam."

"He might be right there."

I slumped against my chair. "Guess the best part of my story was the beginning." I sat forward a little. "However, the second run in with Chaz—"

"Chaz?" Cade asked.

"I think it might be short for Charlie."

"It's definitely short for something." He waved his hand. "Go on," he prodded again.

"I was inside the bookstore talking with Esme when Chaz and his friends—oh, did I mention, they're all part of the Nature Quest Photography Club. Well, they were in the bookstore and *Chaz* (I was using more emphasis on the name to add drama to my story) threw a perfect toddler-style tantrum because his book, some decade-old tome with pictures, was not on the shelves. He insisted Esme order some copies immediately."

"I used to have a friend like that. Avery would throw himself on the ground, crying and kicking and screaming just because his mom refused to buy him a car."

My face popped up. "A car? Like a toy car?"

"Nope, a 1968 Mustang convertible. He was sixteen at the time."

I scrunched up my face. "That seems weird."

"It was quite a sight, I assure you. And now that you bring up the photographer's tantrum, I'll tell you the reason I asked you here."

"Sounds intriguing." I sipped some coffee before it got cold. The sun was shining outside, but there was no way to deny the nip in the air. Especially in the big, drafty house.

"It was probably more intriguing before I heard about the vainglorious Chaz. The photography club is offering free lessons and tips on taking great nature photographs. I signed up, and I was hoping you'd join me."

As much as I didn't relish another run in with *Chaz*, an adventure out with Cade was always entertaining. "I don't know much about photography," I confessed.

"That makes two of us. But we live in a place that is literally nature at its finest. The other day, five elk wandered onto the property. They stayed for an hour, grazing, napping, head butting each other, all the things that elk do, and all I got was this lousy picture." He picked up his phone from the table, scrolled through it for a second and held up a very distant photo of an elk's rear half.

I laughed, then quickly covered my mouth. "I'm sorry. I

take back what I said about my photography skills. I'm Ansel Adams compared to you."

He put the phone down and picked up his coffee. "Hurtful but probably true. The thing is—a year ago, I told myself I would become a budding superstar behind the lens. I bought myself a fancy camera with numerous attachments. That's when you know it's fancy. The thing has been sitting in its case, untouched. It mocks me when I open the case."

"It mocks you?"

"That's right. I'm determined to pull the ole girl out this week and give the whole thing a try."

"Your camera is female?" I asked.

"Thought it was obvious when I mentioned the mocking thing. What do you say, Ramone? Up for a little hiking and adventure with *Chaz*?"

"Well, he is almost entertaining in his quest to be ultra-obnoxious. Sure. I could do with some pointers too. The whole Ansel Adams comparison might have been an exaggeration. I've been known to get just an animal's rear end too."

Cade sat back with a nod. "I think the two of us make a great team when it comes to fun and adventure. Did I mention we have to be up at the trailhead by seven in the morning?"

This time it was my turn to squint an eye his direction. I pointed at him as well. "See, that was a detail that should have gone at the beginning of the conversation."

"Come on, pal. Pretty soon you're going to have to climb out of bed in the middle of the night to prepare all manner of pastries and sweet treats for those of us still tucked in our quilts."

"That is why I'm sleeping late these days. I know, eventually, I'm going to be cursing myself for starting a bakery. Especially when the temperatures are below freezing and I'm out shoveling the front steps at three in the morning. But I think I can make it. I'm looking forward to spending the day with you. Be prepared to spend a long morning with Chaz, award-winning author, at least in his head, prize-winning photographer, that part might be true, and professional snack shopper."

A sharp breeze kicked through the property. The nearby cottonwoods shed a hurricane of leaves and some of the left-over tufts of summer cotton. The debris fluttered down, coating the patio outside the kitchen doors.

"I realized just the other day that this entire property is surrounded by cottonwoods." Cade drained his coffee cup. "My old neighbor, Norbert, used to obsess about falling leaves. He'd take his leaf blower and stand on the roof to keep guard and make sure none of the debris fell on his roof. And that was in the middle of a windstorm." Before I could call his bluff Cade held up his hand. "Scout's honor. The wind would kick up and Norbie, that's what I called him, though we weren't friends—"

"Possibly because you referred to him as Norbie," I suggested.

"No. Do you think?" He actually gave it some thought. "I thought it was a step up from Norbert, but now that you mention it—" Cade shrugged. "Anyhow, he really did stand up on the roof with his blower. Like a dragon spouting fire to keep away the enemy. It was quite the scene. My biggest worry was that I was going to witness Norbie's demise. His roof was steep. One good gust could have been the end of him."

"At least his roof would've been clean when the coroner came to pick him up." I stared down at my empty cup. "This conversation got really weird. Are you sure that was just hazelnut coffee?"

He raised his hand again. "Scout's honor."

"Were you ever a scout cuz I'm not picturing it."

Cade shrugged. "I don't think you have to be a scout to use it."

I nodded. "Yep, I'm pretty sure that's how it works."

Cade stood and picked up the cups. "That's why I like you, Ramone. You call me out on all my baloney."

"Glad to do it." I sat back and watched as he poured us each another cup. He was a strikingly handsome man, and it seemed the two of us had really bonded. But I was confused. Were we just friends? Was this my new kind of adult crush? Most importantly—was the adult crush reciprocated? Why was I having such a hard time reading this whole thing? Boy, I was really out of practice.

four

· · ·

THE SECRET WITH SHORTBREAD, I'd discovered in
my early baking days, was to not overwork the dough. The
butter should be cold but not as cold as for a pie crust. Hands
needed to work fast to get it all incorporated without making
the dough tough. I'd sprinkled coarse sugar on top of my
shortbread rectangles. I placed four sugary, flaky rectangles
on a plate and waited for Nana to return from her walk.
Afternoons were much shorter, and today, a lively breeze had
kicked up to reshuffle the landscape. There was nothing Nana
loved more than a brisk walk on a blustery day. She'd even
pulled out her pale blue knit scarf, an embellishment she
usually saved for winter.

I stared down at my treats. They were in the traditional
Scottish shape, long rectangles with an array of tiny holes,
poked with a fork, to keep the cookies from pillowing or
cracking. I'd decided I would leave half plain and dip the rest

in melted dark chocolate. Tonight was my trial run. If all went smoothly, I'd have my first batch baked, dipped and wrapped for their Saturday morning debut at the store.

I walked to the front window and looked out. The pale blue of Nana's scarf stood out amidst the flurry of gold and orange leaves being whisked about by the wind. The wind in Ripple Creek came in three forms—playful and nippy, the kind of wind that might knock your beanie forward or send a hurricane of dandelion tufts across the lawn. It could be sharp and terse, cold blasts that smacked you and made you duck down to avoid the brittle slap. Those winds were generally explosive and short-lived. You avoided trees with big branches. Then there was the kind of wind like we were having this afternoon, brisk, slightly teasing but, above all, insistent. Cottonwoods tended to be the main target of that last kind of wind. The trees were always too tall for their feet, as Nana liked to say, and their multitude of mini branches snapped clean off to litter the landscape.

I hurried to the door to open it for Nana. A gust swept through right then nearly yanking the door from my hand. Nana's knit hat lifted off her head and took off. I pushed out the screen door and ran after it. Suddenly, I was a kid again, laughing wildly as I chased after a runaway hat. The knit cap bounced and rolled. I was no match for the wind. Behind me, Nana laughed as I raced after it, hopped over the jutting tree root in the front lawn and finally managed to pounce on the hat with one grand leap.

I snatched it up, like a mom grabbing her unruly child's sweater.

Nana was on the phone as I returned, which made the whole event far less triumphant. "Yes, dear, we'll see you soon." She hung up and reached out for her cap. There was a shoe print on the edge of it. "Did you have to step on it?"

I sighed dejectedly. "The alternative would have been throwing my entire body on it, so yeah, I had to step on it. Who were you talking to?" I asked as we stepped inside and shut the door. The interior of the house seemed especially peaceful after the wind outside.

Nana spun around. "Guess what today is?" she asked excitedly, ignoring my question.

I knew exactly what the twinkle in her eyes meant. I shook my head. "No, it can't be that yet. We've only just had our first blustery day. If you start it too early—"

"It's Soupageddon!" she cheered, again ignoring me.

I nodded, knowing there was no point in arguing. Soupageddon was the day when our meals were taken over by soup. Not all, of course. There would be the occasional hamburger or plate of pasta, but Nana's Soupageddon meant she'd be pulling out her special soup recipe box, and, for the foreseeable future, we'd be sitting down to hot bowls of soup. Not that I was complaining. Nana's lentil, sausage and kale soup was the stuff of dreams, especially when accompanied by yeast rolls. But it seemed she started on her soup cooking kick earlier and earlier each year.

"As I've told you, Button, there is no set date for Soupaggedon. It's just something I feel in my bones." I finished the last four words with her because it was a phrase I heard every year. She removed her scarf. "I think we'll start the season with a creamy tomato soup."

"All right, but before you hurry off into your soup-filled world, could you taste my shortbread?"

"Yum, yes. Let me just hang up my things." She draped the long scarf over the coat rack and put the shoe printed beanie on the top of the hook. Nana hummed with pleasure as she bit into a chunky piece of shortbread. She closed her eyes. "Makes me think of bagpipes and kilts and the Scottish Highlands. Perfect, Scottie, really. Oh, could you bake some rolls to go with the soup? Maybe some of those soft rolls with parmesan and thyme."

"I better start them now, so they have time to proof." I pulled my favorite bread mixing bowl out of the cupboard and went to the refrigerator for the yeast and parmesan. "You never said. Who were you talking to on the steps?"

I leaned into the bottom cabinet for the cheese grater.

"That was Dalton."

I came up too fast and smacked the back of my head. "Ouch."

"Oh, Button, you need to be more careful."

I rubbed the back of my head and put the grater down harder than necessary on the counter. One of my biggest fears was that Nana would spill the beans about the mad, crazy crush I had on Dalton in my early years. She wouldn't do it to embarrass me. She'd just blurt it out there in casual conversation because she thought the crush was cute. And while I should have been able to withstand the embarrassment of the secret getting out (it was, after all, years ago) I didn't want

Dalton to know. Now that we lived in the same town, it was easier between us to be two people who had gone to school together and who'd formed a mutual friendship. "Why were you talking to Dalton?"

"It wasn't about you if that's what you're worried about," she said as she pulled tomatoes out of a basket.

"Yep, that's exactly what I was worried about."

She clucked her tongue. "Not everything is about you, Button. I ran into Dalton earlier in town, and I told him Soupaggedon had started. He still remembered it, and he told me my creamy tomato soup was his favorite."

I turned to look at her. "You didn't?"

Nana looked at me with an innocent bat of her lashes. "At least this time you won't be dressed in a t-shirt with a rat's nest on your head. He'll be here at six, so hurry with those rolls."

And there it was. The flutter in my stomach that reminded me I still hadn't shed the remnants of that ridiculous school-girl crush.

five

. . .

THE BUTTERFLIES TOOK a short breather while I busied myself making rolls, but the second a knock sounded on the front door, they returned energetically. Dalton's deep voice floated through the living room and into the kitchen where I'd stayed behind for no other reason except I needed the darn butterflies to settle down.

"Hey, Evie, thanks for inviting me. I've been looking forward to it ever since you asked."

I took a deep breath. I realized Dalton and I hadn't seen each other in at least two weeks. We'd both been busy with work, and while the town was small, we'd somehow managed not to run into each other.

I stepped around the corner into the front room. Dalton was still wearing his official dark green parka, the one he wore once the weather took a turn. And up here in Ripple Creek, a turn was never just around a corner. In Ripple Creek, the weather made an abrupt U-turn. Today's blustery chill was proof of that. It was also assurance that summer was officially over.

Dalton's smile caused a new butterfly dance. This one was a sort of dramatic tango. Hopefully, they'd slow down and end the show altogether once we sat down to dinner. "Hey, Scottie, long time no see. You must be busy with bakery plans."

"And you must be busy chasing down bad guys and keeping the peace on the mountainside." I reached for the coat he'd just removed. "So, you heard the news about Soupaggedon."

"He was the first to hear the big announcement," Nana reminded me.

Dalton nodded proudly. "Guess it was my lucky day."

Our walk to the kitchen was cut short by Dalton's phone. He groaned in irritation. "Excuse me. I've got to answer this. I'll be right back." He dashed outside.

I headed into the kitchen and snuck a few glances toward the front yard through the kitchen door. Dalton was pacing. He seemed agitated. I couldn't make out the words, but he was speaking loudly and tersely to the person on the other end.

Nana cleared her throat. "It's not nice to eavesdrop."

Guilt pulled me away from the window. "If only I could eavesdrop. All I hear are angry mumbles. I wonder if he's talking to—"

"His fiancée," Nana finished for me. "Passionate conversations can happen from both ends of the spectrum. You speak passionately in anger if it's someone who is important in your life. I think we can both assume he's talking to Crystal."

I happened past the window once more and peered up. I had to yank my face away when Dalton inadvertently turned in my direction. "I think you're right."

"She's a high-maintenance gal, I'm sure," Nana said. The tiniest smile had formed on her lips. My grandmother had settled on a silly notion that Dalton would eventually break up with Crystal and then coming riding in on his horse to sweep me off my feet. I told her she watched too many late night, black and white movies.

The front door opened. I rushed to the counter to look busy buttering rolls. Dalton's smile had vanished, and a far more serious but still just as handsome face appeared around the corner.

"Everything all right?" Nana asked casually.

Dalton put his phone in his pocket. "Just the usual day-to-day obstacles. The soup smells delicious." It was a clumsy, abrupt change of topic, but I couldn't blame him. I was sure the last thing he wanted to do was talk to Nana and me about his fiancée. Darn it.

We were several spoonfuls into our soup when Dalton brought up the visiting photographers. "A photography club arrived in town this morning. They picked up a permit to camp up at Blue Jay Ridge. It's a great time of year for that. It doesn't get much more scenic up here than the middle of a beautiful autumn."

"I couldn't agree more," Nana said. "I took a walk this afternoon, and my head snapped side to side to take in the colorful scenery. Some people consider the leaves a nuisance, but this world would be a dull place without those amazing colors of fall." Nana lifted the basket of yeast rolls for Dalton. "Aren't Scottie's rolls delicious?" she added.

"I figured these came from those finely trained hands." He looked pointedly my way.

"Glad you're enjoying them. Speaking of the camera club, I'm heading up to the Blue Jay Ridge trailhead at seven in the morning. The club is giving a lesson in taking nature pictures, and since there's nature all around us in abundance, I've decided to take advantage of their expertise." I'd stolen Cade's sales pitch about the whole idea. I'd also, subconsciously perhaps, left out the large detail about tagging along with Cade for the fun.

"You didn't mention that to me," Nana said. She seemed a little miffed. Unfortunately, after moving back home, I'd somehow lost a grip on my independent adult life. When I was living in the city, I didn't have to check in with Nana to tell her my everyday moves. Now that I was back home, she considered it only polite that I let her know where I'd be at every moment of the day. (Well, maybe not every moment, but close enough.)

"I only just decided it this morning after I met the club members." A small white lie. I was back to my teen years, apparently, and teen years always meant a flurry of little white lies. Not me, of course, but my friends told them as often as I changed my socks. That was mostly because Nana was far more tolerant of teenage behavior than my friends' much younger parents.

"Speaking of the club members," Dalton started. I knew by the amused twinkle in his eye exactly where this was going. "The head of the club was an interesting man."

"If by interesting you mean conceited, full of himself and what was the word Cade used—" I tapped my chin. "Vain-glorious."

The twinkle was gone. Dalton nodded. "Yes, I thought so too," he said quietly. "You're still friends with Rafferty?" he asked between sips of soup.

I straightened to meet the tension head on. The first time Cade and Dalton met was at a murder scene that happened to be on Gramby Estate. To say that the meeting was not cordial was a vast understatement. I could honestly say that I'd never seen two people take such a quick and decisive disliking to one another.

"Why wouldn't I be friends with Cade? He's interesting, charming and, at the risk of sounding superficial, handsome. Three of my favorite traits in men." Even though the topic had caused some tension at the table, Nana was enjoying herself, smiling discreetly into her soup.

"That's fine. None of my business," he said in a tone that seemed to indicate it was indeed his business. He plunged his roll into the soup and took a big bite of it. He chewed it slowly as he stared at me across the table. I met his judgmental stare with a counter stare that I liked to think conveyed defiance. (Admittedly, without a mirror it was hard to tell. It might just have been a crazy, googly-eyed stare.)

"Dalton, how are the wedding plans?" Nana smiled again. "I'll bet you're so excited about the big day." My grandmother would have been great in war. She knew exactly when to lob the grenade. And it hit its target.

Dalton's jaw twitched ever so slightly, and there was a noticeable flare in his nostrils. He'd since pulled his gaze away from mine and was pretending to be quite intensely focused on his soup. "It's fine. Crystal is dealing with all that. I'm too busy."

"But surely she keeps you posted about all the plans," Nana prodded. I slid my foot across and tapped her shoe, hoping she'd get the message. She got it but then I forgot it was Nana sitting across from me. She tilted her face up innocently toward Dalton. "I never had a big wedding or a wedding at all, for that matter, but I'm sure it must be terribly exciting."

Dalton nodded and kept his focus on his soup. "You've got one of the words right," he muttered.

"What's that?" Nana asked. She knew too well what he'd said and what he meant by it.

I was still miffed at Dalton for questioning my friendship with Cade, but I needed to step in. "How long are the photographers camping up there? I talked to one of the members. He's anxious to see an eagle. I had to let him down."

Dalton took a deep breath, relieved to have moved on from the wedding topic. "Actually, I've seen an eagle hanging out at the pond that's west of the trail about halfway to the top. Kentucky and I rode up there last weekend, both days, and he was sitting in the tallest spruce on the north side of the water, waiting for his supper to swim past."

"Good to know. I'll let the club know when I get up there."

"You never said," Nana piped up again. "Who are you going up there with?"

I swallowed a bite of roll and looked up to find both of them looking at me. "Uh, well, I'm going with Cade."

We'd come full circle right back to square one. And they claimed soup was a comfort food.

six

. . .

CADE WAS WEARING a pair of khaki pants, hiking boots
and a zipped up black jacket. He had what looked to be a
pretty impressive camera bag slung over his shoulder. He'd
pulled a black cap low. It caused his longish, thick hair to
nearly touch his shoulders. I'd opted for jeans, hiking boots
and my favorite sweater. It had the amazing ability of not
getting too warm on a hike but providing just enough
warmth if a brisk wind kicked up. We'd agreed to meet at the
trailhead after I woke up late. I blamed my alarm, but it was
more likely the many times I smacked that very same alarm
to silence it. How on earth was I going to get up to run a
bakery?

"You made it, Ramone," Cade quipped. "Wasn't sure you
would." He lowered his sunglasses and looked at me
pointedly.

"Hey, I'm only fifteen minutes late. Got ready in record

time as verified by my hair being swept up in this messy thing that was supposed to be a ponytail."

Cade looked at my hair. "I like it. Goes just right with the adventurous day. As long as no birds mistake it for their nest, all should go well."

"Is that what they call a backhanded compliment?"

"I meant it sincerely." He flashed his white smile.

I pulled my backpack higher on my shoulders. Nana had made two peanut butter and banana sandwiches for me to take along to finish my full transformation back to my childhood years. Peanut butter and banana sandwiches were my favorite, and frankly, they were perfect for a day like today. No refrigeration needed and they provided a nice burst of energy. I'd tucked some of my shortbread into a plastic container as well. I wanted to get Cade's opinion. After all, this was going to be my first big debut at Roxi's. I wanted to make sure it was good.

We'd both parked in the small dirt clearing about fifty feet from the trailhead. Ours were the only two cars aside from the photography club's van. Cade glanced around. "Looks like we might be the only people attending this class."

"I'm not terribly surprised. You'll find that if you live in a place where having an elk peer through your front window is a common occurrence, you don't have much need for pictures. It's all happening in real time."

"And yet, I will not be deterred in my quest to become a superstar with a camera." Cade adjusted his backpack and camera strap. I had no such equipment to drag along, but I hoped there would be tips on taking photos with a phone.

We reached the start of the trail where the list of dos and don'ts told people how to behave on the trail. One of the more unnecessary drawings showed a foot stepping directly on a curled-up rattler with a big red line across it.

"Oh look"—Cade pointed to it—"And I so wanted to step on a rattlesnake today. Guess I'll save that bucket list item for a less restrictive hike."

"You make light now, but just wait until you've stepped off your front porch and missed one of those fanged beasts by inches. Talk about your life passing before your eyes." I shivered as the memory came back in full color.

We started along the trail. It was a nice, easy, meandering and well-groomed path. However, it got a little steeper and more rugged near the top.

"I need to hear the snake story," Cade said.

"I don't know. It wasn't one of my finest hours."

"Now I really need to hear it."

"Fine. Let the humiliation flow. I'd just gotten a new pair of sandals and was racing out to show my friend, Marcy. She'd wanted the same pair, but her mother refused to buy them. Naturally, being twelve, I wanted to rub my good fortune in her face by prancing over to her house in my shiny, new sandals. I hopped cheerily down the front steps and saw the movement out of the corner of my eye." I shivered again. "Everything about snakes—just—" Another shiver, energetic enough to rattle my backpack. My shortbread was going to be shaken to dust by the time we reached the top. "I missed stepping on that horrid rattle end by inches. I decided, long after my heart rate had finally returned to normal and the abject horror of seeing a snake had subsided, that I'd gotten my dose of bad karma for the day."

"Did you prance over to Marcy to show off the sandals?" he asked.

"Of course I did. I was twelve. The snake didn't bite me, after all."

Cade laughed as he pulled the strap of the camera bag higher on his shoulder. "I don't know how you women do it, carrying your purses around all day. I'm already tired of this camera bag."

"Well, *we women*," I started succinctly.

Cade nodded. "Yep, I deserved that."

"We women," I continued, "don't understand how *you men* can leave the house with only your wallet. The purse is an entirely practical invention, and men resort to wallets only because they know the purse is a far better choice but they don't want to admit that women are right."

Cade's nicely chiseled jaw moved side to side in thought. He hadn't shaved this morning. The dark stubble looked good. "I've never heard that theory before, but you might be right."

"In addition, we don't generally carry heavy cameras around in our bags. Your *purse* is extra heavy."

We headed around the curve where the path began its slow ascent to the top. Two mountain bikers were heading down. We stepped off to the side to let them pass.

"Nice day for a hike," one of the bikers said as he nodded his thanks to us.

Cade looked around. "He's right. It is a great day for a

hike. The sky is an azure blue, and the trees, well, can you ever say enough about trees?"

"You know, I don't think you can. I'd say trees and chocolate are two of earth's most precious gifts."

As we hiked around the next bend, the side of the hill fell away and gave way to a mostly unobstructed view of the small pond where Dalton had seen the eagle.

"Oh wait." Without thinking, I grabbed Cade's hand to slow him down. There was no way to deny a nice little spark of electricity exchanged between us. At least I'd felt it. Maybe Cade hadn't. In which case, I was once again being silly when it came to men. Or maybe not. Cade smiled down at my fingers wrapped around his wrist. I released them quickly. I'd almost forgotten my reason for stopping him. "I've been told, by a friend, that a bald eagle has been hanging out near this pond." I decided the detail on which friend was unnecessary. Cade usually had the same bitter lemon reaction to the mention of Dalton that Dalton had whenever I brought up Cade.

"I have yet to see an eagle since I moved in at the estate." We both moved closer to the edge where the best view could be had.

"We're looking for the tallest spruce on the north side." I pointed. "That one."

"Your friend is very specific. How does Braddock know that the eagle will hang out in the same tree?" he asked.

"They're creatures of habit." I realized seconds later that he'd already uncovered the mystery friend's identity. "How did you know I was talking about Dalton?"

Cade shrugged. "I figured otherwise you would have filled in a name. Anyhow, I don't see an eagle. Let's keep moving."

We continued up the trail.

"You know, Ramone, I don't mind that you're friends with the ranger. You don't have to hide it."

If only that were the case with Dalton, I thought wryly.

"I wasn't hiding it. I just didn't supply the name." It was a lie, of course, and I marveled at how well Cade knew me already. Sometimes, it felt as if we'd known each other for years.

A weak breeze ruffled through the trees with enough force to rain leaves down on our heads. A giggle followed.

Cade looked at me. "Did you just giggle?"

"No." I looked back behind us. The trail was empty. "I thought it was you but then something tells me your giggle would be more of a chuckle."

"I don't giggle or carry purses just to solidify the fact that I am, in most respects, manly."

This time it was my giggle. It was followed by the other giggle. It was coming from farther up the trail, and it sounded decidedly flirty. The source of the giggle became apparent as we turned the next bend. Fiona and Allen had left the trail, one of the *don'ts*, to be alone under the shade of a tree. They were standing very closely together, close enough to kiss. When they realized they were no longer alone on the trail, they stepped back from each other abruptly. Fiona giggled again only this one sounded more nervous than flirty.

"I just don't understand how I lost that earring," Fiona

said loudly. It was quite the act. Especially since, from my vantage point, I saw an earring dangling from each of her pert little ears. "Thanks for your help, Allen." The forced tone continued. Now Allen joined in the act.

"Sorry we couldn't find it, Fi." Allen looked our way. "Oh hey, guys, coming up for the photography lesson?"

Cade patted his camera bag. I immediately noticed Fiona's gaze had latched onto my handsome trail partner. "Armed and ready," Cade said. Fiona laughed. It was as fake as the last few minutes.

"We should get back there too, Fiona. Sorry again about the lost earring."

"But you have one in each ear?" (Yes, I was a stinker.)

Fiona's green eyes rounded, and her pretty pink lips formed an "O." She reached up and tugged each earring. "Right. Well, I lost a different one yesterday on the hike up the trail. Shall we head up? I'm sure Chaz is anxious to get started."

Cade waved his hand with a flourish. "After you two."

Allen and Fiona shuffled ahead of us. Guilt sure could take the energy out of your step. Not that they needed to worry about us. Cade didn't even know what the whole thing was about. Naturally, I needed to let him in on the juicy details. Once again, I took hold of his hand to slow down our pace and put some distance between us and the pair.

Cade smiled cockily down at my hand on his wrist. "If you want to hold my hand, Ramone, just ask. I'm all for the woman making the first move."

I dropped his hand and gave him a light knuckle in the

arm. "I'm not trying to be forward," I hissed quietly. I tilted my head up the trail toward the other couple. "I've got gossip," I said again through my teeth.

"Gossip, you say?" he said loudly enough that even the bears already in their winter dens could hear. He laughed. "Sorry, it was too easy," he said as he leaned closer and lowered his voice. "I'm all ears."

"Well, it all feels kind of anticlimactic now, but—"

"Those two are not supposed to be canoodling under a tree because she's dating one of the other club members," Cade guessed.

I stopped short on the trail. He walked a few extra steps and looked back in question.

"You sure know how to ruin a juicy piece of gossip. How did you know?"

"A lucky guess. She's obviously a flirt. She practically undressed me with her eyes, and we'd only just met. He looked pleased with himself for having been caught under the tree with her. Only, he also looked slightly terrified. It was a mix of pride and fear. From there, conclusions were drawn."

"You think you're very clever, don't you?" I teased.

"I'd say so, but that's just one clever man's opinion." Other voices drifted toward us, and the distinctive smell of a campfire wafted through the air. We were nearing the campsite. Allen was suddenly walking toward us. "I'll be right with all of you. I spotted an interesting lookout location, and I wanted to go back and check it." He hurried past. Fiona, on the other hand, continued on toward camp.

Cade leaned over. "Do you want another clever man's opinion?"

"Always."

"That man did not want to show up to camp with the woman, and that was why he told us his long, rather ridiculous excuse for turning back."

"You really are clever," I said.

"See, told you this would be an enlightening adventure."

seven

. . .

CHAZ WAS LEANING over the campfire stirring scrambled eggs in a skillet. "Welcome. We're just about to have some breakfast and then we can head out." Surprisingly, there were three other people, not of club affiliation, sitting around the campfire. They had their shiny new camera bags. One man, who was tucked into a lot of layers of clothing, was balancing a tin plate of eggs on his legs as he drank from his water flask.

Chaz offered us plates of eggs. Cade decided to partake, but I'd reheated one of Nana's waffles to eat on the way to the trail. We sat down on the low benches around the campfire. Chaz was wearing a crisp flannel shirt (not an easy shirt to make look crisp, but he managed) pleated pants and a yellow knit scarf tossed jauntily around his neck. He struggled to keep it from falling into the eggs and, for that matter, the campfire, but he seemed determined to keep wearing it. A small white badge glinted in the sunlight. It read *Chaz Voorman, President.* He certainly took his position seriously.

He piled eggs on a plate and handed them to Cade but not without first beaming at him. "I can tell you I was excited to hear that the well-known author, Cade Rafferty, would be joining us. Big fan." It was interesting to see Chaz impressed with someone other than himself. Just as soon as the nicety was finished, he leaned over and looked past Cade. "Shayla, I told you not to use that lens today. It's far too bright out."

Instinctively, everyone at the campsite turned in Shayla's direction. She looked utterly embarrassed and quickly ducked back into her tent with the camera. Everyone was still looking that way when Allen came wandering out from the trees. He looked stunned and, frankly, a little distraught that everyone was looking his direction. He'd missed the first few moments and had no idea we'd been looking that way for a different reason. The earlier look of guilt returned. Allen's gaze flashed to Fiona. She pretended to be busy securing her nametag.

"Allen, there you are," Chaz said. "Where have you been? We're almost out of eggs. You'll have to make something else for your breakfast." After he finished, he looked pointedly in Fiona's direction. I was no expert, but something about the look he gave her told me Chaz was more clued in than the secret couple realized.

Cade leaned so close our heads tapped together. "And the plot thickens," he muttered. The *look* hadn't escaped my friend either.

"When you promised a fun adventure, is this what you had in mind?" I asked.

"If I'm being honest—no. This is just the powdered sugar on top." Something caught Cade's attention over my head. "And here comes the moldy cheese to ruin it."

I laughed. "What?" I looked back over my shoulder. Dalton had ridden up on Kentucky. He was wearing his official uniform, so this wasn't just a casual trail ride. I turned back to Cade and shook my head.

"Ah, Ranger Braddock," Chaz said. "Can we interest you in some breakfast?" Chaz was certainly a charmer when there were other people in the vicinity. Though, it was all so fake, it was hard to categorize as charming. Poor Shayla was definitely not considering it that. She'd emerged with a different, smaller camera. Rather than hang out at the campfire, she carried a thermos with her to the far end of the clearing to be alone.

Dalton dismounted and walked Kentucky toward the group. Fiona hurried over with the pretense of petting the horse, but her sparkly eyes were trained on the man leading the horse. "Are you here for some photography lessons?" she asked Dalton with a slight tilt of her head.

"No, I'm just making sure everything is going all right up here. Remember to douse that campfire thoroughly when you walk off to take pictures. We're still in fire season."

Chaz nodded. "I'll see to it myself, Ranger Braddock."

Dalton looked across at me. His eyes landed there for long enough that a few of those butterflies kicked into gear. When his gaze moved to Cade, he glowered for a brief moment before turning away.

"Your *friend* doesn't care for me sitting here next to you at this campfire. I'm tempted to put my arm around your shoulder just to irritate him more."

I got up and gave Cade my own glower. The last thing I wanted was to be a pawn in their inexplicable man war.

Cade looked properly chastised. "What? I said I was tempted. I didn't actually go through with it."

I headed across to where Dalton was standing.

"Ah, come on, Ramone, don't be mad," Cade called. Dalton heard every word. His glower returned.

"Just coming over to say hi to Kentucky." I stroked the horse's neck. "I didn't know you were coming up here this morning."

"It's part of my job," he said curtly.

"Of course." I patted the horse's neck a few more times. "Well, I guess I'll see you around."

"I guess so, *Ramone,*" he said dryly. I flinched. I never minded when Cade called me Ramone, but I didn't like it coming from Dalton. Might just have been the way he said it. He was mad I'd come up to the campsite to spend the morning with Cade. Nana insisted their rivalry stemmed from their mutual attachment to me, but given my track record with men, I found that notion not only hard to believe but outright comical.

I breathed a sigh of relief when Dalton climbed back on his horse and turned the gelding toward the trail. It seemed I was holding my breath in his presence, yet again. Only this time, it was for an entirely different reason. I hated the tension between Cade and Dalton. I considered both to be my friends, but it seemed one day, I might have to choose. That left me feeling entirely unsettled.

I returned to the campfire. Chaz was busy doing his Smokey Bear duty making sure the breakfast fire was smothered. Cade had taken his camera from the bag to get ready to start the morning.

"Fancy, fancy," I chided as I reached him.

He gazed at me for a long moment. "You're not mad at me, Ramone, are ya?"

I bit my lip in thought. "Let's just say I'm not *not* mad."

"Oh man, I know I'm in trouble when she's slinging double negatives my way. I promise to do better." He bowed politely.

"I'm holding you to that promise."

eight

. . .

IN THE FIRST hour of the hands-on photography lesson, where angles, light, composition and all the other buzz words from high school art class were tossed about, I realized I was a baker and most definitely not a photographer. Cade, on the other hand, listened raptly and seemed to be absorbing as much information as possible. I was having more fun people watching. The dynamics of the club were interesting to say the least.

"Shayla, again, you're only going to get a bleached white photo of sunlight." Chaz was never pleasant or patient when he criticized his club mate. She always seemed to take it to heart. It amazed me how calm she stayed in the face of such harsh treatment. I'd have thrown my camera at the man fifteen minutes into the lesson. As it was, he wasn't directing his mean comments at me, and I wanted to throw my camera at him. Of course, that would include my phone, and I'd already run out of replacements on my phone insurance. (The hazards of working in a fast-paced restaurant kitchen.)

While the more serious photographers were gathered at the edge of the trail, a place with a great vista and a treacherous drop-off, I decided to stroll back to the campsite and nibble on a sandwich. The campfire had been doused properly. The only thing remaining was a touch of the smoky scent it was still giving off. The smell took me back to campfires my friends and I used to have up at the very same site. When we were finally old enough to hike up to Blue Jay Ridge alone, four or five us would arm ourselves with flashlights, graham crackers, chocolate and marshmallows and have a full-on giggle fest around the fire.

Four tents, two nice, top-of-the-line models and two that looked a little more second-hand, circled the campsite. The group had come prepared with folding chairs and tables, a large ice chest and a locking box to store dry goodies that a bear might find tempting. (In my experience, that was just about anything.)

I was glad to have a few minutes to myself. I enjoyed being with Cade, but I needed a few minutes to mentally debrief about this morning's unfortunate event. That and there was something so irritating about Chaz's pompous tone (oh that was it—the pompous-ness) that I needed a break from his voice.

I sat on one of the benches and was busy searching my cavernous backpack for a sandwich when I heard giggling coming from one of the nice tents. I already knew the giggle. It had a distinct fluttery sound as if Fiona had actually practiced making her giggle extra flirtatious. This time a deep laugh joined her. I knew Chaz was out on the trail giving everyone pointers.

I took my mind back to the last half hour or so. Come to think of it, I hadn't seen Fiona or Allen for a long time. I surprised myself. They were part of the main event in my people watching escapade. I caught at least three brushes of the hands and shoulders, two secretive smiles and, at one point, Allen brazenly placed his hand on the small of her back. Chaz was so enamored with his own voice and expertise he didn't seem to notice any of the intimate exchanges.

My hand finally made contact with the parchment wrapper on my sandwich, but it seemed I was intruding on something and it had nothing to do with photography. I dropped the sandwich back into my bottomless pack and got up from the bench. I hurried back to the trail. As much as I sort of relished the idea of catching the two of them coming out of the tent (especially after the awkward show they put on earlier) I decided I'd had enough drama for one morning.

I followed the sound of Cade's laugh and then realized, with a start, that I already easily recognized his laugh. Cade had broken off from the group and joined Kevin at another place on the trail. I reached the two men. They were discussing Kevin's work. Both men looked up from their phones as I approached.

"Ramone, I wondered where you'd gotten off to," Cade said. "Kevin was showing me his work. It's amazing." He held his phone up for me to see. There were some truly beautiful examples of nature photography, some with animals and some without.

"These are fantastic," I added. "It looks as if you've been to some exotic places. How on earth did you get so close to lions?"

"A very long camera lens and a very fast jeep." Kevin pulled a pack of cinnamon gum from his pocket and offered us each a piece. I turned it down. I'd geared my taste buds up for Nana's delicious peanut butter and banana sandwich. I didn't want to shock them with a bite of cinnamon.

"Kevin has been giving me some pointers," Cade said.

"Pointers without all the attitude," Kevin noted. They both laughed.

"Your club president does take himself very seriously." I already knew exactly how Kevin felt about Chaz. He'd spoken quite clearly about it in the bookshop.

Kevin chuckled at my comment. "You could say that. Not sure if I've ever met anyone who was so self-confident and, at the same time, not the least bit self-aware."

Cade nodded. "Couldn't have said it better myself, and I only just met the guy."

"Well, that's a compliment to me," Kevin said, "knowing how well you say things. I'm looking forward to your next book."

"Leave me with an address, and I'll make sure you get a signed copy."

Kevin's face lit up. "Really? That'd be awesome. And I'll send you a signed copy of that Grand Canyon photo you liked so much."

It seemed there was quite a bonding fest happening. I decided to find another quiet place to eat the sandwich. My stomach had expected lunch, and it wasn't giving up on the idea. "I'm going to leave you two to it and get started on something I'm exceptionally good at—eating. I'll catch up to you later." I headed back up to the campsite, then remembered why I left it in the first place. I turned off on one of the smaller paths to look for an altogether more peaceful place to enjoy my sandwich.

nine

· · ·

I'D GENEROUSLY GIVEN my second sandwich to my ill-prepared adventure mate. That left both of us with empty stomachs by the time the lessons were over, and we had to hike all the way back to our cars. We made a plan to meet up again under the neon light of Emmet's Diner.

Cade was taking a photo of the diner when I pulled into the lot. I climbed out of the car. "I guess you're feeling pretty professional now that you've had lessons," I called as I crossed the lot to him. I was feeling and surely looking bedraggled with messy hair, a sheen of dust everywhere and the tired tromp of heavy feet. Cade, on the other hand, looked exactly the same as he had this morning, before we'd taken even one step on the trail.

"Feeling a tad bit more skilled than I was when I woke up this morning, but I doubt magazines will be clamoring for my work just yet." He was still wearing his camera bag on his shoulder. He carefully replaced his camera into the bag before snapping it shut. He tapped it gently. "Now then, are we ready to clog our arteries with diner food?"

"Speak for yourself," I said. "I always order the spinach salad."

"Really?"

A laugh spurted from my lips. "Gullible." We headed toward the entrance.

"See, I didn't take you as one of those bird nibblers." He opened the door for me, and I strolled inside. My senses were immediately overwhelmed with the aroma of grilled onions, cherry pie (Emmet's specialty) and hot coffee.

The hostess waved us through. We were between peak hours, so there were plenty of open tables. We chose one near the rear of the restaurant and next to a window.

Cade plucked the menus out of the stand and slid one my way. "I've only eaten here twice. Both times I ordered the chili cheese omelet. I'm thinking a plate of fried chicken today. That photo snapping has left me starved."

"I'm pretty sure it was the hike and the fresh air. The only things getting a workout from photo snapping were your fingers and eyeballs." I rested my hands on the menu. I didn't need to look to know I was getting a turkey club. "What exactly is a bird nibbler, and be careful how you answer because stereotyping is considered distasteful."

Cade closed his menu with a satisfied nod about his fried chicken decision. "Now, I'm not sure I should elaborate. Stereotyping is sort of built into the narrative. However, in my defense, is it really stereotyping when I can say I've witnessed it with three women? I mean, that's a pattern, don't you think?"

"That depends. Witnessed what?"

"Bird nibbling. For example, Date A, I'll keep names hidden to protect the privacy of the bird nibbler, ordered a steak and lobster. The most expensive thing on the menu, I add unnecessarily to give weight to the claim that I'm not a cheapskate on dates. She took, and I kid you not, one bite of steak, three chunks of lobster, no butter, another unnecessary detail, but you see where this is going. She took a bite of her salad, then leaned back and sighed like my Grandpa Harold at the dinner table and claimed, with no small amount of drama, that she was full. When the waiter suggested she take the rest home to enjoy, she insisted she couldn't eat another bite of it because she was so full from the dinner. Of course, I told him I'd be taking it home."

"You do realize that Date A went home immediately afterward and devoured a bag of barbecue potato chips and a pint of Ben and Jerry's Cherry Garcia?"

Cade squinted one eye at me. "Isn't that a form of stereotyping?"

I shrugged. "No, because I've done that myself. That's why I had those specifics ready to go."

"Yeah, I wondered about that. Anyhow, I was under no illusions. I was also angry enough that I bid her adieu and never called her again." Our server put down some glasses of water and took our order.

"Did you actually literally bid *adieu*, cuz if so, she was probably just as glad you didn't call."

He laughed. "See, Ramone, that's why I like hanging out with you. You get me. And excuse the bragging, I think I get you."

The conversation had turned in an unexpected direction. Was Cade about to suggest we take this friendship further? Did I really want that? I wasn't entirely sure. Was my indecision and confusion based solely on the long-held truth that once romance enters a friendship the whole thing falls apart at the seams?

I was intrigued. I sat forward and took a few gulps of ice water. "What do you think you get about me because, frankly, I envision myself being a complicated, mysterious and not-easy-to-read type."

"Complicated maybe. Mysterious." He scrunched his face up for a second. "Highly overrated, in my opinion. I've found —" he paused. "Spoiler alert. Stereotyping about to take place. In my opinion, mysterious means the person hides the fact that they have huge mood swings and that most of those swings tend to be on the negative side. I don't think that's you at all, Ramone. You say it like it is, and I like that."

"Touché, my friend with very few filters." We clinked water glasses.

"Now that we've got the deep discussions behind us—" I put a napkin on my lap in anticipation of my turkey club. "I haven't told you the interesting part of my morning, and it had nothing to do with photography."

"Is that so?" He leaned one arm along the back of the vinyl seat. Emmet's Diner was a typical last century diner with vinyl seats, some of which were in bad need of repair, harsh lights hanging from chrome pendants and a tile floor that was crisscrossed with scuff marks. Emmet himself only worked the night shift. He liked to be in charge during the hours when shady or rowdy characters were more likely to step inside. People packed the place at midnight for some of his more popular breakfast specials. I'd done the same many times as a teen. Now, I couldn't imagine eating pancakes at midnight let alone being wide awake at that time.

"While you were busy learning the ins and outs of awe-inspiring nature shots, I ended up in a little 'call of the wild' scene of my own."

My analogy didn't quite do the trick. His brow arched. "You met up with a wolf?"

"No, I guess that was too vague. I walked back to the campsite to eat a sandwich, and there was giggling and deep laughter coming from one of the big, fancy tents."

It didn't take him long to decipher my meaning, even after my silly analogy. He lowered his arm and sat forward. "Was it the same pair we caught making out under the tree? I wondered where those two wandered off to."

"I didn't stick around to see exactly who came out of the tent, but I recognized her giggle. I could hear Chaz and his pompous baritone down on the trail, and you were with Kevin, so I can only conclude Fiona and Allen were at it again."

"And you're sure Chaz and Fiona are an item? I didn't get much sense that they were a couple or, for that matter, even had admiration for each other. She kept telling him he was going too fast, and he kept sniping back about her inter-rupting too much. Both accusations were true."

"I sensed they were a couple at the market and bookstore. But maybe I misjudged it."

"However—" Cade paused as the server placed the food down. He smiled and nodded at her and then continued once she walked away. "Even if they're not a couple, and you prob-ably had it right when you saw them at the store, Allen and Fiona acted as guilty as two kids who'd just cheated on a math test when we came upon them on the trail. Why would it have to be such a secret unless they were cheating on someone?"

"Good point and why did they wander off today to be alone at the camp?"

Cade grinned slyly. "Well, it's hardly easy to be romantic in a tent when you're surrounded by other tents."

I quickly picked my sandwich up to hide the blush that had heated my face. Unfortunately, my clumsy attempt at camouflage didn't work. Still, Cade was gentleman enough not to mention it and to change the subject.

He took a bite of his mashed potatoes. "Hmm, just like great granny used to make."

"Did you actually know your great granny and eat her mashed potatoes?"

"No, I hardly knew my grandmother. She had my mom at thirty-nine and my mom had me at forty. Lots of old people hanging out when I was born."

I sat up a little straighter. "Who's calling forty old?"

He plowed another forkful into his mouth. "Hmm, so good."

"Smooth," I said. The sandwich was tasty. I was a few bites in when I noticed Cade had not touched his chicken or biscuit. "You know, you could have just ordered a side of mashed potatoes and gravy?"

"No. You're kidding? Darn." He picked up his glass for a toast. "Here's to hanging out with a friend who gets ya."

I toasted back. I gazed at him over my glass of water. This whole thing was more complicated than I realized. Just where were we heading? I supposed it didn't matter as long as we got to hang out and have fun together. Maybe I was over-thinking the whole thing. Maybe having a good friend, who just happened to be male and attractive and witty, was all I needed right now. After all, I had a big year ahead of me. I was about to open a bakery. I didn't need any of life's other complications to get in the way of that. I needed to stay laser focused on my business.

ten

. . .

I WAS ashamed to admit I was exhausted after the long morning of fresh air and hiking. The turkey sandwich might also have contributed to my need for a nap. But after a quick snooze and a shower, I was up and ready to make four batches of shortbread for Roxi's market.

Our neighbor, Hannah, was sitting at the kitchen table with Nana for their usual afternoon cup of coffee. They both stopped a conversation rather abruptly when I entered. They also both wore that guilty look that your coworkers wore whenever they'd been talking about you and you nearly caught them at it. Not that I'd ever had that happen. Well, maybe once or twice, but in my defense, as head pastry chef, I occasionally had to be the bad guy.

"Is that why my ears were burning?" I quipped. Then it occurred to me what they might be talking about, and I felt a defense was needed. I poured myself some coffee. "I'm not going back to the old days of soap operas and nacho flavored chips. I was just tired from the hike."

Nana looked confused. "What? We weren't thinking that. I figured it had been a long morning up on the mountain, and I heard your alarm several times this morning"—she peered up pointedly—"so I knew you'd be tired."

I poured some cream in my coffee and turned back around with my cup. I caught the tail end of a clandestine look exchange.

"You two are as subtle as a town crier in the middle of a library. What's up?" I pulled up a chair. The shortbread could wait. Something was afoot, and I was determined to have the beans spilled. I sat, cradling my cup of coffee and giving them an expression that said *talk*.

Hannah looked gingerly at Nana. She needed permission from the big kahuna first.

"It's yours to tell, Hannah." Nana shrugged as if it all meant nothing to her, but the fact that Hannah was guarding whatever the secret was until she was given the OK assured me it was significant.

Hannah wriggled a little to center herself on the kitchen chair. I was expecting something huge, something earth-shattering for all of a second, then I remembered in late summer when Hannah had stumbled into our house, horrified and out of breath and all because the statues on the Gramby Estate had been vandalized. I lowered my expectations accordingly.

Hannah sipped some coffee for dramatic effect or fortification. It was hard to tell which. Her slightly hunched shoulders lifted and fell with a deep breath. Yep, it was the drama thing. Although, a deep breath could have been fortification too. The important thing was that it was taking her so long to tell her tale, I had time to analyze all her gestures. I was predicting something as mundane as the mailman mixed up Hannah's mail with the Hannah over on Ridge Road.

"There's trouble in paradise," she said with thespian level skill.

I looked at Nana, hoping she would chime in and fill in a few details. For example, what kind of trouble and exactly where was this paradise. Nana had her lips rolled in, either from amusement or to keep herself from rudely running roughshod over Hannah's story. Hannah did seem excited to tell it. I just hoped it would get better and a little more in-depth.

Hannah took another sip of coffee.

"I'm not following?" I said it as a question in case I was supposed to understand exactly what she meant.

"Well, now, this whole thing comes from a reliable source, but I did not witness any of it personally. Still, Gretchen Small's niece, Hayley, told Gretchen and then Gretchen told Isabel, her neighbor, and I happened to run into Isabel at the market and she told me."

I raised one brow at her. "So, the reliable source is Hayley or is it Isabel? Long chain there, Hannah, but now you have my curiosity piqued."

"Hayley works up at the Miramont Resort. She runs the reception desk. Apparently, one of the visitors had his car broken into. The windshield was smashed, though nothing was stolen." Hannah waved that comment off as unnecessary. "The man was irate, and he told Hayley he needed to talk to the manager. They called Crystal Miramont. As you know, she's running the place most of the time. Naturally, she called the ranger, who, as we all know, is her fiancé, Dalton Braddock." Another superfluous detail. "Apparently, it took Ranger Braddock three hours to get up to the resort. Hayley was still behind the desk for those three hours, and she said Miss Miramont kept pacing through the lobby angrily to check the parking lot." I briefly wondered if the incident had happened while Dalton was up at the campsite. "When Ranger Braddock did show up, Miss Miramont made quite the scene. They were still yelling at each other after they moved the *scene* outside." Hannah sat back with a satisfied smile. "And that's why there's trouble in paradise."

I knew very well that Nana was watching me the entire time to gauge my reaction to the news. I didn't even need to look her direction to know she was wearing a sly grin. But I had no intentions of fortifying her crazy notion that someday I'd end up with Dalton Braddock.

I nodded and gave my own dramatic pause with a sip of coffee. Both women were watching me now. I raised my brows. "Is that all? I'm glad it wasn't anything too terrible like a murder. We had enough of that this summer." Not that I didn't have a slight itching for another case to solve. Internally, I was doing a bit of a happy dance, but my voice of reason was reminding me that couple spats were common, especially before a big wedding. "I'm sure they're just experiencing pre-wedding jitters." I took another sip of coffee to show just how unflappable I was about the whole thing. "John and I couldn't seem to agree on anything for months before the wedding. I slept in the spare room for three days after we argued about which brand of toothpaste to buy."

Nana cleared her throat. "If you're using you and John as weight to your argument, may I remind you how that all ended."

I hated Nana when she was being clever. I stood up. "Anyhow, I've got dozens of shortbread cookies to bake. I'll leave you two to your chat."

eleven

· · ·

ROXI ROLLED out two open shelf display cases and set them in a place that could not be missed if you were at the checkout counter. I'd wrapped two cookies in cellophane and tied each pair of treats off with a small curling ribbon.

"These looks so fun and yummy," Roxi said as she held up a bag with two chocolate dipped cookies. "I think I'll buy one for my lunch."

"Please, partner, you don't need to buy one. Take as many as you want. I think I might have made too many." I glanced out the front window. "The town seems quiet this morning."

"It's still early. These beautiful fall vistas are luring people up the mountain. We'll sell out by the end of the day, you'll see." Roxi smiled past me at someone coming in the door. "Ranger Braddock, can we interest you in some delicious shortbread?"

I turned slowly, reprimanding the butterflies to quiet

down. I held up a bag. "I think we can give one to the man who keeps our town safe." Dalton looked less than happy this morning. "Everything all right?" I asked. Naturally, I was replaying what Hannah had told me over our cups of coffee the day before.

Dalton nodded and pushed his sunglasses into the top pocket of his shirt. He took the cellophane wrapped cookies. "These look delicious, Scottie. I'll have them with my lunch." He was low energy, depressed almost. Nothing about him seemed right. I also got the sense he wanted to talk about it but not in front of Roxi. Dalton wandered sort of aimlessly and ended up at the cold drink section. I finished my display and put the basket I'd carried the shortbread in behind Roxi's counter. Roxi must have picked up on the same vibes as me.

She leaned down as I was pushing the basket under the counter and out of the way. "I'm no expert, but I think that boy needs a good listening ear and a friend's shoulder to lean on," she whispered.

I nodded in agreement. I pretended to put the finishing touches on the display while I waited for Dalton to pay for his bottle of iced tea. I followed him out. He heard the door behind him.

"Oh, hey," he said quietly, "are you heading home or are you going to wait around to see if your cookies are a hit? Not that there's any question about that. I know people are anxious for your bakery to open."

"I was heading home," I said motioning toward my car. "But first, I thought I'd take a detour to find out why my friend is so blue." I looked up at him. "Anything you want to talk about?"

Dalton shook his head. He'd pulled on his sunglasses, so it was harder to read his thoughts. "No, I'm all right."

"That declaration did not sound the least bit convincing."

The side of his mouth tilted up, the side that always produced his single right cheek dimple. "You always did know me too well. I still remember when I got in trouble in Mr. Trumble's fifth-grade class. I was upset about it all day because I'd been accused of something I didn't do. My friends, even the one who'd actually stuck a felt-tip marker in the pencil sharpener, went right on with their day, having a blast at recess and laughing and joking around about the tongue-lashing I got. I was sitting on that bench that was under the mulberry tree."

"Yes, the one with all the bird poop," I added.

"That's the one. What did we call it? The pigeon rest stop? Anyhow, I was there feeling extra sorry for myself, and there came little Scottie Ramone in a pair of shiny black boots that were too big for her feet."

I covered my face. "Don't remind me." I dropped my hands and laughed. "I loved those darn boots. Thought I was a real go-go dancer."

"They were pretty cool," Dalton said. "I could tell you were really proud of them. You walked over, your ankles turning this way and that in your chunky boots, and you sat next to me. You didn't say a word because you knew talking about it would only be humiliating. You handed me an oatmeal cookie wrapped in a napkin."

I smiled at him. "I remember that. I'm just surprised you do. You were, after all, Dalton Braddock, and I was just *little* Scottie Ramone."

He was shaking his head before I could finish. "It's sad but I can count on one hand how many times someone was genuinely nice to me, when someone made me feel a hundred times better with a small gesture. And you were never just little Scottie Ramone. You were always a bright light at school. Funny, pretty and always sympathetic when someone else was having a bad day."

I was nearly overwhelmed by his unexpected words. "That's nice to hear, Dalton, and you were always a person I considered worthy of giving my oatmeal cookie to."

We stood there silent for a second, with only the breezes through the trees and the occasional passing car to punctuate the quiet. His gaze held mine for a long moment, then a car honking in the distance broke the spell.

"When you ended things with your fiancé," he started out of the blue. "How did you know it wasn't going to work? When did you realize you needed to end it? Was it one thing? Or a whole string of them?"

I was done being overwhelmed and was now more than a touch stunned by what he was asking. Did Hannah's story hold more weight than I realized? Was there actually trouble in paradise?

I tucked my hair behind my ear as I gave it some thought. It didn't take all that much reflection. "It was a string of things, but mostly, Scottie Ramone was slowly being erased and replaced with the woman who was Jonathan Rathbone's future bride. John kept trying to mold me into his idea of the perfect wife, and I kept realizing I didn't fit the mold... at all. Then that scary weekend when Nana went missing and her neighbor was strangled, I got absolutely zero support from John. I needed it that weekend, but he was only worried about how my abrupt absence looked to his relatives and coworkers. He was also dead set against me starting my own bakery even though he knew it was my lifelong dream."

"Why was he against it?" Dalton asked.

"I don't know. Mostly because it wasn't going to spring a nice tidy profit from the get-go. New businesses always take time to land in the green, especially a bakery. John was all about money." As I said it, he flinched.

"I'm not marrying her for money," Dalton said. "Of course, having money and not needing to worry about it is a bonus. After my parents packed us up for the city, we struggled financially for a long time. They never said anything to me, but I knew we were eating boxed macaroni and cheese three times a week for a reason. I saw the toll it took on my mom and dad, and I'm happy to not have that burden for my own marriage. But that's not why I asked Crystal to marry me."

"I'll be totally honest, Dalton. I was shocked to find out you two were engaged. I knew both of you growing up, and I never would have pictured the two of you together. That said, I'm sure you'll be happy." I shot the addendum in quickly when I realized I was sounding jealous. (Which I was, he just didn't need to know that.)

Dalton adjusted his sunglasses and glanced casually around. "Yeah, I'm not so sure about that." He said it quickly and quietly almost as if they were words that weren't supposed to spill out. "When we first started dating, it was just fun, laughter, all the cool stuff that comes with a new relationship. I convinced myself Crystal had changed and very much for the better. She was carefree, sweet, even humble. I'm starting to worry it was an act."

All I could think was Crystal Miramont acting humble was a red flag of giant proportions. The girl I grew up with didn't have a shred of humility.

"Dalton, I'm not going to give you advice on this because, frankly, it would be highly biased advice, which is never good advice."

His brows bunched together. "Biased?" he asked.

I realized too late that I'd, as the saying goes, stepped in it. But I had a way out other than confessing my undying love for the man. "It's just, I considered you a friend in school and growing up. Crystal Miramont did not fall into either of those categories."

He seemed to accept my explanation. "I guess Crystal did sort of run in her own gold-lined social circles back then."

"You could say that."

Dalton's two-way radio buzzed. He pulled it off his belt. "This is Braddock. Over." I couldn't help but sigh a little at the sound of his official voice.

"Ranger Braddock, we have a report of a missing hiker up near Blue Jay Ridge, over. A male, thirty-nine years old. Up visiting the area with friends."

"Right. I'll head up there now. Keep me posted if you hear word back that they've found him."

"Blue Jay Ridge?" I asked. "It might be someone from the photography club. I can go with you."

He was about to say no.

"Dalton, I know those trails as well as anyone. I'll be two more eyes on the search."

He put the radio back on his belt. "Can you follow with your car? If this goes late, I'll have to get a team out there. You'll need a way to get back to town."

"I'm right behind you, Ranger Braddock."

twelve

· · ·

KEVIN AND SHAYLA were waiting for us at the trailhead. Both looked worried and fatigued. Shayla was nursing the water from her thermos as if she'd climbed Everest. The elevation and dryness were quick to cause dehydration if you weren't used to them.

Kevin met Dalton as he stepped out of the truck. "It's our club president, Chaz Voorman." He lifted his phone. "Here's a photo from yesterday morning. We spent the day taking photographs, grilled some burgers and beans, then we went to our tents for the night. It took us a few hours to notice him missing this morning because we all slept late."

"Is there any chance he left for home without telling anyone?" Dalton asked.

Kevin pointed out the club van that was still parked in the dirt clearing. "We all drove up here together, and the van is still here. Besides that, he'd started the pancake batter."

"Right. Where are the others?" Dalton asked.

"Everyone else is back up at the campsite. We spent the last hour going up and down the trail. There's no sign of him. He was an experienced hiker. We all travel a little off the trail now and then if we see something particularly photo worthy, but we also know the rules are 'don't wander off too far and always let someone else know where you're going.' None of it makes sense." Kevin rubbed his hands together in angst. "I think something has happened to him."

Dalton took off toward the trail, and the rest of us followed like an entourage. "Has anyone tried calling him?" he asked as we passed the corny little warning signs that showed feet on a designated trail to keep people from getting lost.

"I did," Shayla piped up for the first time. I'd observed on more than one occasion that she was the quiet, reserved one of the group. She'd taken two of Chaz's harsh lectures calmly, without a response or defense. "It went right to voicemail."

"I tried calling him right before you arrived," Kevin said. "Same thing. Straight to voicemail."

"Scottie, why don't you head up to the campsite and help the others look around up there. There's that big boulder about five hundred yards to the east—"

"The one that if you stand up on it and yell you get a nice echo off the next mountain? I know it," I said. "Good place to stand and take a picture."

"Exactly. Check out the place where the snow melt trickles through the mountainside. The one we used to say was the mountain taking a—" He cut it short since we were in mixed company. "You know the place."

"I do."

"I didn't get your names," Dalton said to the others.

I hurried ahead while introductions were completed and search instructions given out. Dalton and I had both spent a lot of time on the trail and at Blue Jay Ridge. It was a hangout place for kids in the summer. We knew all the secret nooks and places a person might wander off to.

When I reached the campsite, Fiona was sitting on the low bench around a cold campfire pit being comforted by Allen. Not surprising. Fiona looked visibly distraught. Allen, not as much. He looked up quickly when he heard me step into the clearing.

"I thought you might be Chaz." He just as quickly removed his arm from Fiona's shoulder. It was a clumsy attempt to hide that they'd been intimate, just like when we caught them under the tree. "We seem to have lost our president."

Fiona whimpered into her tissue.

He patted her on the arm. "Don't worry, Fi. He'll show up. Chaz knows a lot about the outdoors and being in the wilderness. I'm sure he just followed some bald eagle or an elk so that he could take one of those award-winning photos. You know he'll do anything for the right shot."

Fiona lowered the tissue. Her nose was red and her hair was disheveled. The gray sweater she was wearing was a few sizes too big. I surmised that Allen had lent it to her since he was only wearing a t-shirt. "That's just it. He'll stop at nothing. What if he wandered too far off the trail?" She glanced around. "He could have fallen into a ravine or broken his ankle on a rock. It's a big mountainside, and there are so many trees. And wild animals…" She sobbed into her tissue.

I could see that I wasn't going to get much assistance from Fiona, and Allen seemed loathe to leave her alone in her state of distress. I had at least two destinations to check before making my next plan.

I marveled at my sense of direction. I'd stood on echo rock (our very imaginative name for it) at least a dozen times, yelling out my name and pretending to be Tarzan, but it had been years since I'd been there. I remembered the general direction. After the small worn path had disappeared beneath debris, other landmarks, like the tree split in two by lightning and the stump that had many initials carved deep into its rings showed me the way. It wasn't long before I'd reached the big granite boulder. Its mostly flat surface had been worn even smoother through the years.

I walked a wide circle around it. "Chaz? Chaz, are you out here? Everyone is very worried." No response and no sign of the club president. I climbed up on the rock to get a better view of the surrounding area. "Chaz!" The only answer came from the echo.

From the giant rock, it was a short hike across to the side of the mountain where snow melt trickled through the granite. A deep, very narrow chasm ran up the length of the cliffside to a small concave ledge above. Snowmelt always collected in the shallow basin. From there, it ran into the open seam where it dribbled out near the bottom. There was always a large puddle on that section of trail, and the rock was mossy-green along the chasm. The second destination was also a bust. No sign of Chaz. I called his name a few times with no luck.

I decided to head back toward the campsite. Maybe Fiona had recovered. She and Allen could join me for a wider search of the area. I assumed if we didn't find Chaz in the next hour, Ranger Braddock would call in a proper search team. There had been plenty of lost hikers in the woods above Ripple Creek over the years. Generally, a thorough search ended happily. But if the person was gone too long, there was danger that they'd wandered off even deeper into the landscape, or worse, fallen and hurt themselves.

Fiona was drinking from her water flask. She looked marginally better than when I first arrived at camp. Allen was pacing the site, which did the search effort little good. He looked up again, briskly and hopefully, as I stepped into the clearing.

"Sorry, just me again. No word from the others?" I asked.

Allen shook his head. "Nothing. What could have happened to him? How does a grown man vanish into thin air?" He waved toward the table with their food and cooking supplies. "He started the pancake batter this morning. None of it makes sense." His words made Fiona cry again.

I stood in the middle of the camp and swept my gaze around for the next logical direction to head. A glint of something shiny stopped my visual search near the far edge of the camp. The campsite was mostly a flat clearing, perfect for setting up tents and tables. But once you passed the farthest point of the camp, there was a narrow path that had a sharp and, in some places, treacherous drop-off. There was a warning sign not to get too close to the edge because of loose rocks and the occasional burst of wind. The photography club had taken advantage of the views from that side of the camp the morning before. Occasionally, a gliding hawk or an energetic V of geese would fly over the deep valley below the edge. It was a great place for photos.

I headed toward the tiny piece of shiny paper that fluttered like a silver fish that had been pulled from the water. As I got closer, it became clear that I was looking at the foil wrapper from a stick of gum. An edge of it had gotten jammed under a rock, and the free end vibrated in the breeze. I snatched it up and took a whiff. Cinnamon. Kevin had been chewing sticks of cinnamon gum when Cade and I joined him for the lesson. I jammed it in my coat pocket. I was busy telling myself it had gotten free of the trash bag or from Kevin's pocket when my eyes caught something else. It was yellow fabric.

My heart sped up as I inched cautiously toward the edge of the trail, well past what was considered safe given the drop-off below. The breath caught in my chest as I peered down into the ravine. The yellow I'd spotted was a butter yellow knit scarf. It had gotten caught on the thorny shrub growing on a rocky outcropping. It waved in the breeze like one of those inflatable characters car dealers used to draw attention to their lot. Its long fringe-ended arm kept waving wildly as if it was trying to point something out. I had to inch even closer to the edge. Gravel and dirt flowed down the side of the cliff below me. I spotted his arm first. I leaned to look past the first rocky outcropping. My worst fears were confirmed. I'd found Chaz Voorman. It seemed this search was not going to have a happy ending.

thirteen

. . .

DALTON HAD CALLED the mountain rescue team to get
help down to Chaz, but we both knew from the way he was
lying—face down, sprawled, and frankly, a little *broken*—that
no help was needed. Chaz Voorman had died from his fall.
Unfortunately, he'd landed in a place that was nearly impossible to get to without the rescue team. They lowered two
men and a basket down to the ledge where Chaz lay. Shayla
had taken a hysterical Fiona into a tent to rest and get out of
the sun. Allen and Kevin stood nearby the action, consoling
each other and looking plenty distraught. They seemed to
sense, too, that Chaz was beyond help. No one could easily
survive the fall he'd taken. Now, the question was—how did
the tragedy happen? Dalton was keeping his thoughts to
himself as he waited for confirmation that Chaz was dead.

The basket and the rescue team reached the top. I waited
on my own, standing between Chaz's club mates and the

group working on the victim. From the grim expressions, it was easy to conclude what was already obvious—Chaz had not survived the fall.

Dalton was on his radio for several minutes as the rescue team packed up their equipment. The rescue team truck was purchased with rugged climbs in mind. The trail was just wide enough for an emergency vehicle to get up the mountain. It was going to be more challenging for a coroner's van to make it up the hill.

Dalton spotted me standing alone in between the action and the grieving friends. He adjusted his sunglasses back onto his face as he walked over. "I'm sure I don't have to tell you the bad news." He glanced toward Allen and Kevin. They seemed reluctant to walk over and hear the dreadful truth. The two women were still in the tent. It seemed everyone had already figured out the ending to this accident.

"What are you thinking, Ranger Braddock?" I decided a time like this required his official title.

"I'd say the guy got too close to the edge and slipped. I nearly lost my footing a few times myself. I'm going to have a safety barrier put up across that section of the trail. I know people get angry when we add something manmade to the scenery, but if visitors are going to be taking pictures or selfies over that ravine, they need to know there's a limit on how far you can step out."

"The camera," I muttered to myself. "He wasn't wearing a camera."

Dalton glanced over at the long basket holding the body.

"You're right. Just a second. I'll go ask the crew if they saw a camera." Dalton walked away.

Allen and Kevin approached me cautiously. "Is it true?" Kevin asked. "Chaz is dead?"

"I'm afraid so. I'm very sorry," I said.

"What on earth was he doing out on that ledge?" Allen asked. "He wasn't usually so careless."

Dalton returned and nodded politely to the two friends. "Gentlemen, I'm sure you've heard the terrible news. I've contacted the county coroner, and he's making his way up the mountain as we speak. Would the two of you like me to break the news to the women?"

Allen shook his head. It looked heavy on his shoulders. "No, it'll be better coming from us." He took a deep breath. "Well, Kevin, we should let them know now. Fiona has already been in a state this whole morning." Allen looked at Dalton. "They were a couple, you know."

"I didn't realize. Give her my condolences."

I found the last part of the conversation somewhat ironic, especially coming from Allen. But this wasn't the time for gossip. First, we needed to figure out how a perfectly fit and, by all accounts, skilled hiker managed to slip off the side of a cliff.

Allen and Kevin headed toward the tent where the women were waiting for news. Their steps were heavy, and their heads hung low. It was never easy delivering the news of someone's death, but this one was so wholly unexpected, it would make the task harder.

"Something just occurred to me," I said as soon as the men

were out of earshot. "If Chaz slipped, why was he face down?" I mimicked slipping down a hill with my feet going out in front of me. That would send my body backward. "Wouldn't he have landed face up?" I was sure I'd added an intriguing layer to this whole thing, but Dalton didn't look too impressed.

"Unless he hit that first ledge, the one where the shrub snatched his scarf, and that impact sent him forward. By then, he would have lost his grip on gravity. His body would have been sailing through the air."

"Yeah, you're right. For a second, I thought maybe Chaz hadn't merely slipped. I thought possibly he died by more nefarious means. A push or something."

Dalton was suddenly intrigued. "Hold on, now that you mention it, he did land far out in the ravine. Even if he clipped that first ledge on the way down, if he slipped, how did his body get hurtled so far from the cliff?"

"Unless he jumped," I added.

Dalton glanced over at the body. "Hadn't even considered that. They said he'd gotten up to start pancakes. Why would someone come up here with a social club to commit suicide?"

I shrugged. "Maybe he got up thinking he was feeling good enough to make pancakes and then those dark thoughts that cause people to kill themselves took over. I agree, though, strange timing. And there wasn't anything about his countenance yesterday that made me think 'gee, that man's suicidal.' He was all bluster and bragging and bossiness."

"Sometimes big personality traits are covering up depression. An act of sorts to throw people off. But we're jumping to a lot of conclusions. I'm going to talk to his friends. They might have more insight into his mental health."

"Good idea. And let's not forget the third possible explanation of how Chaz Voorman ended up in that ravine. Someone might have given him a push. If it was hard enough and the assault was unexpected, it would be a plausible explanation for how he ended up so far out from the cliff's edge."

Dalton lifted his glasses up and half-smiled at me. "You're looking for a murder, aren't you? I can see that little investigative twinkle in your eye."

I placed my hand lightly on my chest and dropped my chin dramatically. "Why, Detective Braddock, what are you insinuating? That I'm some sort of ghoul who thrives on murder mysteries?"

He crossed his arms and tilted his head. "I probably would have left out the word ghoul, but yeah, something like that."

fourteen

. . .

A CLOUD of dust was followed by tires grinding over the trail. The coroner had arrived. "Guess we'll know more soon." Dalton went off to greet the coroner's team.

Allen emerged first from the tent. Shayla followed looking a little shaky but not too distressed. Kevin stepped out next. Fiona didn't leave the tent.

I joined the three. It was time to get some information on the club president. "How is Fiona doing?" I asked.

"She took a sleeping pill to rest," Shayla said.

I looked around the site. There were four tents and five campers. "Excuse me for asking, but was Fiona sharing a tent with Chaz?" I realized I should have prefaced my question with a little more context. The three looked slightly taken aback.

"I hardly see how that matters." Allen was the first to bite my head off, but the others looked equally perturbed.

"I apologize. I didn't make myself clear. I'm not trying to be nosy. It's just the ranger and I were wondering if there was a chance, any chance that—" I paused. It was harder than I realized to bring up the notion of suicide. It was such a sad, dark subject. "We just wondered if Chaz had been feeling all right? Was he upset about anything?"

"Do you mean was he suicidal?" Kevin once again proved himself to be the most straightforward of the bunch. He looked at the others. "He seemed his usual self, don't you think?"

Allen nodded along eagerly. "Yes, I'm sure he just got too close to the edge and slipped."

It was an easy explanation, an especially handy one if someone in the group had decided to help him along with a push.

"I'm sure you're right," I said. "I just wondered if Fiona had noticed anything last night when they went to bed. Or maybe she spoke to him when he woke up."

Shayla was shaking her head. "Fiona relies heavily on sleep aids." There was the slightest judgment in her tone. "She told me she took one right after she got into the tent and was out cold until this morning when she heard the three of us outside. She didn't see or hear Chaz get up or leave the tent."

"At least that's what she's telling us," Kevin said with a good dose of skepticism.

Not surprisingly, Allen stepped up to defend Fiona. He literally stepped forward too, chest slightly puffed and hands balled at his sides. "Just what are you insinuating, Sanderson?"

Kevin put up his hands. "Cool your jets, Lennon. We all know you and Fiona were seeing each other on the side." (It was hard to see how that follow-up comment would actually help to cool his proverbial jets.)

Allen's chin lifted and jutted forward. His fists grew tighter. "You don't know anything. You're the one who had it out for Chaz. Maybe we should start considering that he didn't slip and fall. After all, Chaz has stood on some pretty precarious mountaintops and cliffs, and he's never had a problem."

It was Kevin's turn to fill his posture with bravado. I was quickly losing control of the situation, and it seemed I wasn't going to get any backup from their other group member, Shayla.

I stepped halfway between them, deciding to err on the side of caution in case a fist was thrown. The last thing I needed was a black eye or split lip. "Gentlemen, it's obvious the shock of the morning has caused both of you a good deal of stress. It's to be expected. But, at a time like this, it's better to provide each other with support. (Apparently, hidden somewhere in my many personality traits was a high school guidance counselor.) Let's not jump to any conclusions."

Kevin shrugged. "He started it with his accusation that I had something to do with Chaz's accident." His statement reminded me of how I discovered Chaz in the first place. A wrapper from Kevin's cinnamon gum was fluttering under a rock near the place where Chaz went over. It placed Kevin at the scene. There was always the reasonable assumption that a breeze picked up the piece of litter and carried it to the place where I'd found it.

"I'm just saying, if anyone had motive—" Allen started.

"It would be the person who was trying to steal Chaz's girlfriend right from under him."

"Allen, Kevin," Shayla said quietly. "This bickering is going to wake Fiona, and it's the last thing she needs. I think the best thing for all of us to do is to start packing up the campsite. We need to keep Chaz in our thoughts. The poor man lost his life this morning. It was a terrible tragedy. We need to figure out positive ways to deal with it." Shayla smiled weakly my direction. I nodded my approval. It seemed Shayla, too, had a high school counselor deep inside.

Dalton came up behind us. "I'm going to need to speak to each one of you separately." His words sparked the flames again. Although, he couldn't possibly have known they would. He hadn't been privy to the last few minutes of conversation like I had. And an interesting few minutes they'd been. I was stunned at how quickly the two men had started accusing each other of murder. While Dalton hadn't given me word yet, the look on his face said it all. Chaz Voorman was murdered, and the suspect list was small, complex and, seemingly, fraught with motives.

fifteen

· · ·

EVEN THOUGH HUNGER was telling me to go home, I
stuck around, more than a little curious to see what the
coroner had to say. In the meantime, Dalton's one-on-one
sessions had caused further rifts in the group. It was as if
each member had gone to their respective corner. The two
men were busy shooting daggers at each other from opposite
sides of the camp. Shayla was Dalton's current interviewee.
She stared up at the handsome ranger with a bit of a twinkle
in her eyes as she quietly answered his questions.

The coroner and his two assistants had taken over the
central crime scene, the last presumable place Chaz had stood
before falling to his death. That left little for this self-
appointed investigator to explore. I tried to stand close to the
coroner's team to grab a few snippets of conversation but
quickly found they silently entered most of the information

directly into an iPad. Whatever happened to good ole conversation at a murder site?

Across the way, movement caught my eye. The tent opened and Fiona stepped into the sunlight, shading her eyes and looking like someone who'd been lost in space for a year and had only just landed back on earth. To say she looked out of it was an understatement. Noticeably, Allen avoided running immediately to her side. Mostly because Kevin had crossed his arms to watch Allen do just that. It would be further proof of Kevin's theory that Allen killed Chaz to have Fiona to himself.

Fiona smoothed her ruffled head of hair back and shuffled toward the campfire benches. She sat down with a hard thump and stared with great sorrow at the activity happening across the way. I concluded she was probably in no real state to talk. Then again, maybe that was the best time to talk to her.

I walked over and sat down next to her. "Can I get you something? Some water?" I asked.

She lifted a small thermos out from her sweatshirt pocket. "I'm fine. Well, not fine, but—" She shook her head sadly. "I still can't believe this is happening. Why are there so many official people standing around? Didn't Chaz slip accidentally?"

"That's what we're waiting to hear. Shayla mentioned you were fast asleep when Chaz got up this morning. Did you hear him or talk to him at all?"

She took a gulp of water. "Not since last night when we went to bed. We were both tired from the long day, and I went out like a light. I took a sleeping tablet. I always have a hard time sleeping in nature." She shivered slightly. "So many creatures out there waiting to pounce."

"They're usually more afraid of us, but that's not important. Chaz seemed like an energetic, full-of-life kind of guy?" I was asking to see if she disagreed. It would make sense that a significant other would see a side of a person that the general public didn't see.

She didn't contradict the statement. "Yeah, that was Chaz. He could be brusque and harsh sometimes, but that was only because he went at life full throttle. He didn't like people or things to get in his way." She pulled a tissue out from her pocket and blotted her eyes. "I can't believe I have to talk about him in past tense."

Fiona knew that Cade and I had happened upon her and Allen while they'd stepped off the trail together. There was no other way to interpret what we saw. She was ignoring that inconvenient detail at the moment and remained fully immersed in her grief over the man she was presumably cheating on.

"Were you together a long time?" I asked. Dalton was finishing up with Shayla. He'd be heading over to Fiona next. I only had a few more seconds to get in some of my own interview.

"We've been off and on for about five years. You know how it is sometimes when you stay together more for convenience than anything else. Both of us dated other people occasionally, but we always ended up back together."

Dalton was heading across. I couldn't stop myself from

tossing out one more zinger. "And your relationship with Allen?"

Her face snapped my direction. Her lips parted in surprise. She'd either forgotten that I saw her on the trail the day before, or she'd assumed that they'd been clever enough to make it look totally innocent. I was thinking the latter.

"Miss Paxton, a word, please," Dalton called before he reached the campfire bench. He shot me a sly look. He knew what I was up to. I felt entitled. I had, after all, discovered the body.

I stood up, dusted off my bottom and nodded to Dalton as I walked away. Hunger was starting to gnaw a hole in my belly. The investigation would have to wait. It was time to get home for some much-deserved lunch.

sixteen

. . .

A HOT SHOWER and one of Nana's grilled cheese sandwiches set me right again. I'd stopped at Roxi's store on the way home to check on sales. While the store had been, in general, pretty quiet for a Saturday, according to Roxi, two-thirds of the shortbread was gone. She'd even had repeat customers on the same day, who'd returned for more short-bread. It gave me a nice little rush, that Chihuahua giddiness, knowing that people were enjoying my baked goods. It was especially nice to know considering I was planning on opening a business that was solely dedicated to selling my baked goods.

I'd taken a hot cup of tea out to the front stoop to reflect on the busy morning. A few wispy clouds, frail like shredded gossamer, had drifted in to blot out some of the bright sunlight. There was a familiar nip in the air, the one that always reminded us that as wonderful as it was to live in

Ripple Creek, winter was not far off. Winter weather varied, but we could count on snow, ice and subzero wind chill no matter the year.

I stretched my legs out, so my heels rested on the bottom step. Enough time had passed to give the coroner a chance to come to a conclusion. I decided to text Dalton.

"What did the coroner say?" I texted.

Surprisingly, he rang me back.

"Hello?" I asked, not sure why he chose the formality of a call.

"Since I'm not actually supposed to hand out official information to just anyone and since I know that one *just anyone* in particular will pester me until I tell her what I know, I decided to tell you verbally. You know, in case the higher-ups get wind of this and ask me for my phone."

"First of all, I do not pester. I can be persistent on certain matters, but I resent being called a pesterer or whatever one who pesters is called. Secondly, I resent, even more, being referred to as just anyone. May I remind you that I lent you pencils almost every day in class. And more than once, I gave you the answers to the math homework." I made certain to always bring an extra pencil to school knowing full well Dalton would be without one. Nana couldn't figure out why she had to buy me so many pencils.

"That's right. I did sort of rely on you for my writing tools. Thank you for that. I guess I owe you."

I brought my feet up to the step below me and rested my free forearm on my thighs. "See, that's better. You do owe me."

"I'll send you a twenty-four pack of pencils in the mail."

"Dalton, spill the beans."

"The coroner confirmed it was foul play. The way he landed, the distance his body flew out over the cliff's edge. His landing, face down, is more consistent with some force from behind rather than his feet jumping off the cliff. There was also one bruise below the shoulder blade that could have been made by a hand and not jutting rocks. The club was supposed to leave tomorrow morning. I've asked them to stick around a little longer."

"How did the interviews go?" I was probably pushing the limit, but it was worth a try.

"I can't discuss that, Scottie."

"That's all right. I hung out with the club the day before, and I spoke to all of them after *I* discovered Chaz's body. Let's just say, sometimes hanging out casually with people gives you insight they'd never share with law enforcement."

"I'm very well aware of that, but if there's anything that could help the case—" Call waiting beeped in on his phone. He paused and a noise that I was sure could be interpreted as a grunt of frustration followed. "I've got to go."

"I understand. When the fiancée calls—" I teased.

"Yeah, yeah, all right. Call me if you think you have anything that might help find out who pushed Chaz off the cliff."

"Sure thing," I said. Even I didn't believe me. I might have divulged some of the inner workings of the group if we hadn't been interrupted by the one person who could turn me sour. I chided myself for letting the very notion of Crystal calling her fiancé get to me. My phone beeped right after I hung up. It was Cade. He was probably the best person I could talk to right then.

"Hey, Ramone, I'm grilling steaks. I figure this might be my last chance before the dreary mantle of winter settles over our fair town. Join me. I have enough to feed a small army."

I texted back. "Are you saying my appetite is that of a small army?"

"Of course not, Ramone. Maybe just a small platoon. Anyhow, if I haven't already messed up my chances for a dinner guest with my inelegant analogy—seven?"

"I do love being part of an analogy, elegant or not. I'll be there. Should I bring anything?"

"Just your wit, your beauty and—maybe a bottle of red wine?"

"I can do that. See you then."

Nana came to the screen door. She'd taken a rare afternoon nap. She looked refreshed. "I forgot to tell you—Hannah invited me for some fried chicken. You can join us if you like." She pushed out the screen door and braced her hand on my shoulder to sit down on the step next to me. She immediately pulled closed her lavender sweater. "Jack Frost is just around the bend."

"Sure feels that way. I've got dinner plans tonight. Cade invited me for steak."

"Oh, I was sure you were talking to Dalton."

"I was but that wasn't about dinner. How did you know I was talking to Dalton?"

Nana's sly little smile appeared. It always caused the lines around her mouth to deepen. "You put on an entirely different voice when you talk to Dalton. I call it your gushing voice because you're practically overcome with joy when you're talking to him."

I laughed dryly but instantly tried to recreate the voice in my head to see if she was right. "We were talking about a murder, so I hardly doubt I was overcome with joy. I think you're hearing things."

"I don't think so, Button." Nana stretched her short legs out. She was only wearing fuzzy socks. She tipped her feet back and forth playfully. "But let's forget about that. I didn't realize there was a murder. How awful? Who and where?"

"It was up at Blue Jay Ridge. A group of photographers were camping there. One of them fell off the cliff and died."

"That sounds more like an accident. Or is that what someone wants everyone to believe?"

"Bingo. The second one... I think. It's hard to know who because, to be frank, the victim was sort of unlikable. He was arrogant and a bully. At least in the interactions I witnessed."

"Yes, but that's not a strong motive, is it? Plenty of people are arrogant bullies, but they don't all get pushed off cliffs."

"There might be at least one solid motive out there. The victim, Chaz, was seeing one of the women, Fiona. By all accounts, Fiona was having an affair with Allen, another member of the group."

"Aha, I see." Like I'd done moments before, Nana brought her feet up to the step below and hugged her knees closer. "I always consider jealousy to be the more noble and romantic motive for murder."

I laughed until I looked over and realized she wasn't being facetious.

"Really. I mean think about it. If you kill someone out of jealousy, then you are truly nuts about the person you killed for."

"Or you're just truly nuts," I added.

Nana laughed. "Good point. Anyhow, so you're going to have dinner with Cade." Another sly smile.

"I am. It's no big deal, just steak and some red wine and, knowing the two of us, a lot of chatter and laughter. He'll want to hear all about the murder."

"Is it going past a casual friendship?" Nana had always been open-minded, progressive, but there were some things I'd rather not discuss with her. She was, after all, my grandmother. Most people's grannies asked things like do you need new underwear for Christmas and whatever happened to that nice friend you used to play softball with. That wasn't my grandma. She got right to the heart of things.

"It's just a friendship." It wasn't a lie. Even though I was thoroughly confused about which way it was heading, for now, it was purely platonic. "Nana, don't forget I just came out of a long-term, tumultuous relationship. Give me some time to right my own boat before I jump onto another."

Nana reached over and hugged me. "You're right, dear. None of my business." She laughed. "Sometimes I forget you're not my little Button anymore but a grown woman."

I hugged her again. "Sometimes, I wish I was your little Button again. Life was much simpler back then." I held her for a few seconds longer. She seemed frailer than I remembered. She was getting older, but I refused to let my mind even consider the possibility that one day she'd leave me for good. I squeezed her tightly before letting go.

She reached up and placed her hand on my cheek. "You're always my little Button. Now go get gussied up for your date."

I shook my head. "Again, not a date." I headed toward the hallway.

"If you say so," she quipped lightly.

seventeen

. . .

I PARKED MY CAR, snatched the bottle of red wine from the seat and followed the aromatic smoke to the back of the big, rambling house. Cade was standing at a grill with a long pair of tongs in one hand and a leaf blower in the other. The purpose of the leaf blower became apparent when a gust of wind sent a flurry of crisp leaves toward the patio and the grill. Cade lifted the blower. It hissed with energy. The leafy debris quickly shifted course and scattered away from the grill, settling, eventually, at the edges of the patio.

I couldn't hold back a laugh as I reached him. "A scene I will never forget. This is taking successful grilling to a whole new level."

Cade bowed slightly. "Thank you. I owe my old neighbor, Norbie, for the idea. The biggest problem is that each gust gets a little stronger, and I fear my weapon of choice"—he lifted the leaf blower—"will soon be rendered useless." He rested the leaf blower down next to the barbecue. "However, the steaks are almost done." He pointed at me and closed one eye. "I had you pegged as a medium."

"I definitely like it well past rare." In truth, I wasn't much of a steak lover at all. I'd said yes more for the company than anything. After Nana's teasing, I'd spent an inordinate amount of time on wardrobe choice. I worried that if I pulled on something too date-ish like a silky dress or snug cashmere sweater, I might end up looking foolish. Then again, faded jeans and a button-down shirt might have given off too casual of a vibe, like hey thanks for inviting me but I couldn't be bothered to dress for dinner. After a great deal of agonizing and way too much overanalyzing, I opted for a khaki pair of pants and a black, semi-tight sweater. Cade was wearing black slacks, slightly more formal. He'd topped the pants with a ski sweater, dark blue with a white Nordic pattern across the chest. There was no denying that he was quite the sight. I just wasn't sure if it was a date look or a hey, I live in the mountains look. Argh, I had to stop trying to figure this out or I'd risk ruining what I was sure would be a fun evening.

"There's a corkscrew in the top left drawer next to the sink," Cade said. "I took out some wine glasses." He spun around from his grill. "You *did* buy wine with a cork?"

"Yes, Mr. Prickelty Snobbington, it has a cork." I walked into the kitchen. Two settings had been set on the small kitchen table. A casserole dish of green beans topped with crunchy onion bits sat next to two foil-wrapped potatoes. I smiled thinking I couldn't remember the last time a man had cooked me dinner. The closest John had ever come was calling for Chinese takeout. And he'd considered himself quite the catch for doing it.

The kitchen was coming together. In fact, I sort of envied the historical ambience of the whole place. It would be wonderful to live in a relic from another time period. You could feel how much life the home had witnessed, the events, both sad and happy. I imagined plenty of laughter and sobs had bounced off the sturdy walls. I opened the wine and poured us each a glass.

Cade was no longer brandishing his barbecue tongs as he carried in a platter with two sizzling steaks on top. "I thought we should eat inside. Otherwise, I'd be required to hold onto the leaf blower. Although, I didn't have time to make a salad, so maybe the leaves could fill in for lack of greens."

"I think inside is nice." Two tall silver candlesticks with long white tapers sat in the center of the table. Candles definitely fell in the category of a date-night dinner but then the lighting in the kitchen wasn't great. Maybe they were there for practicality's sake.

"Have a seat, milady. I shall serve you." He bowed and waved his hand with a flourish. "Darn it, I left the salt and pepper outside."

"I'll get it, *milord*. By the way, did lords of the castle ever say 'darn it'?" I laughed at my joke as I hurried out to get the salt and pepper. By the time I returned, Cade had lit the candles and placed a steak and potato on each plate. He was leaning in the refrigerator and emerged with a dish of sour cream. "I'm afraid we're going old school with the potatoes. I had grand visions of a cheese sauce and perfectly crisp bacon bits, but I realized I had none of the right ingredients. Namely, the cheese... or the bacon."

"Those seem like necessary ingredients for that particular vision." I sat down and placed the linen napkin on my lap. Cade carried the sour cream dish and a pitcher of ice water to the table.

"Tell me, Ramone, what were you up to today while I was toiling over my computer keyboard chewing myself out for being utterly illiterate and unimaginative?"

I adjusted the napkin primly on my lap. "Well, Mr. Rafferty, while you were hunched over your laptop scolding yourself, your friend was up at Blue Jay Ridge searching for Chaz Voorman, the president of the photo club."

A short laugh burst out. "Did that pompous fool get himself lost? Where did you find him?" he asked lightly as he sawed off his first bite of steak.

"Well, you see, that's where this story takes a dark turn."

Cade stopped the knife and looked up at me. "A dark turn? Do you mean?"

I nodded. "I spotted the poor man crumpled, broken and most decidedly dead. He'd fallen to his death off the steep end of the campsite."

Cade sat back, stunned. "I knew I'd invited the right dinner guest. Tell me more. Was it an accident, or did someone nudge the annoying man right over the edge?"

I tried to tamp down my smile, considering the subject matter. "Looks almost definitely that it was the latter."

"No kidding. Well, Ramone, it looks like you've got yourself wound up in another murder case. Who are we thinking for the main suspect?" Before I could answer he snapped his fingers. "That's right. Wasn't there some sort of tryst happening between Allen and Fiona? Did we ever untangle what was happening there?"

"I think I have it pretty well sorted." We paused for a bite or two. "Food is delicious, by the way."

"Thanks."

"Fiona was Chaz's girlfriend. They were on and off a lot according to a very distraught Fiona. And while she wouldn't come right out and admit, it was easy enough to surmise that Allen and Fiona hadn't wandered off that trail to search for a missing earring or anything else, for that matter. Then there was the tent incident—" I blushed bringing it up.

"That's right. You were an unwitting witness to a little afternoon fun."

My blush deepened. "What did you marinate this steak with?"

"Changing the subject, eh, Ramone? That's all right. And it's just salt and pepper, but I suspect you already knew that. What about the other guy. Kevin, right?"

"Yes, Kevin. I suppose everyone at the camp is a suspect. It happened very early while the rest of the group was still asleep."

"Except for the pusher." Cade mimicked a shove.

"I suppose, except for the killer. Ranger Braddock interviewed everyone." I always dreaded bringing up either man in front of the other, and Cade's reaction did not disappoint.

He moved his mouth side to side like someone might do to taste a wine. "Braddock was there?"

"It's kind of his job," I reminded him curtly.

"But you'll find the killer first, won't ya, Ramone? I'm counting on it."

I lowered the forkful of food I was holding and tilted my head at him. "You just want me to beat Dalton to the punch because you want him to lose. It has nothing to do with your dear friend winning."

"Nonsense. Of course, I want my dear friend to win. It's just sweeter when your win means that Braddock loses."

I shook my head and plunged my fork into my mouth.

"All right, all right. It's far more important that you get the win. The rest is a residual bonus."

I swallowed. "You should stop while you're ahead. Actually, you should stop before you dig yourself in deeper is a better way to phrase it."

Cade lifted his glass of wine. "Here's to me shutting up before I'm waist deep in it."

I laughed. It was almost impossible to stay mad at the man. And he looked especially dashing tonight in his ski sweater.

I picked up my glass. "To you shutting up." We clinked glasses and sipped the wine.

"Hmm, good choice, Ramone."

"I *did* work at a Michelin star restaurant. Even though I

was standing in the pastry kitchen, my staff and I occasionally got to sample the various wines."

Cade looked impressed. "I realize there is so much I don't know about you." He lifted his glass. "Here's to finding out more."

We toasted again. He gazed admiringly at me over the rim of his glass. Such confusion.

eighteen

· · ·

NANA'S VOICE and the buttery smell of waffles woke me from a deep sleep. A day on murder mountain, as I was now calling it, followed by a night of wine and lively conversation had left me exhausted. Normally, I would've been having a mental debriefing about the evening with Cade for at least a half hour after my head hit the pillow. But that wasn't the case. Plus, there wasn't that much to go over. We ate, drank, talked and solidified our friendship even more. When Cade walked me to my car, it seemed as if he might lean in to kiss me. That one quick gesture could have put to rest the many questions I had about our friendship. But the kiss didn't happen. I was left feeling a little disappointed and a lot more befuddled.

Nana was talking to someone. I gasped. "Dalton," I said on the release of breath. It was waffle morning, after all. I wasn't going to be caught in my usual Sunday morning state.

I ran a brush through my hair and pulled on a t-shirt and shorts. I sashayed down the short hallway thinking this time I'd dazzle. My posture deflated when I discovered Hannah sitting at the table behind a butter-topped waffle.

"Scottie," Hannah said cheerily. "We thought you might sleep all morning."

"How was the *evening*?" For no reason in particular, Nana put special emphasis on evening.

"It was very nice. We had steak and green beans and red wine." That was all I planned to divulge about the evening. Not that there was much more to say.

Nana turned from the stove with a waffle on a plate. She handed it off. "Hannah was just telling me that she ran into Mr. Rafferty at the market."

Hannah nodded along. "That's right. I was telling Evie that I was highly impressed. Such a handsome and well-spoken young man. And he carried my bag out to the car. Can't believe he lives *all alone* in that big house." We were getting a lot of emphasis on key words this morning.

"I agree, Cade is very well-spoken." I sat down at the table and slathered my waffle with butter. The butter application was my cue to them that the topic was finished.

Nana joined us with her own plate. "I do miss strawberries. They add such a pop of flavor. I'll have to make some cinnamon apples next time."

"Your waffles are so good, I could eat them plain," Hannah said as she added another dose of maple syrup to her plate. "I heard there was big trouble up on Blue Jay Ridge. Theresa, down on Turkey Road, said the coroner van was heading up there."

Nana glanced at me to see if the topic could be discussed. I shrugged. "Go ahead."

"There was an accident." Nana was giving the G-rated version of the event. "A young man fell to his death. That's all we know right now."

Hannah smiled at me over her plate. "Have you seen Ranger Braddock lately?" There was enough tease in her tone to assure me Nana had been filling her in on my history with Dalton. I never minded as long as it was just Hannah, and I knew Nana well enough to know she'd threatened to withdraw waffles, coffee chats and every other pleasantry if Hannah told anyone else.

"I've seen him," I said plainly.

"Did you happen to hear any more about, you know, trouble in paradise?" Nana asked. She was using Hannah's own words in the question, but Hannah looked perplexed. "You know," Nana prodded. "What you were telling us the other day."

"Oh right, about the rift between Dalton and Crystal." She pulled in her mouth as if she had indeed heard more. I sat forward with interest and then wanted to kick myself for doing so.

Nana and I waited patiently as we chewed bites of waffle.

"No, nothing new," Hannah said airily and returned to her waffle.

I fell slightly forward with disappointment. We gobbled up

waffles drenched in syrup and sipped coffee. This was one of those mornings when Nana and Hannah decided to reminisce about the past. I knew it was time to make my exit. I rinsed my dishes and grabbed my laptop. I had research to do.

I knew only superficial tidbits about the victim and the group at the campsite. If Chaz had won awards and had a book published there had to be plenty of information out there about the man. I typed in his name. Oddly enough, the first entry contained his name along with the name Kevin Sanderson. I still had the gum wrapper in my coat pocket. In retrospect, I should have handed it to Dalton, but it seemed like such a small, insignificant piece of evidence at the time. It seemed I was about to find another place where the two men crossed paths other than in the photography club.

I clicked on the article. It was an opinion piece written five years ago by none other than Chaz Voorman. There were a few boasts about his awards and book following the byline—I assumed to give weight to his opinion. The entire piece was about Kevin Sanderson and his "vapid collection of pedestrian photographs." It contained some technical critiques about light and perspective that flowed over my head, but the last line was a doozy. "In conclusion, I find it close to ludicrous that the Metropolitan Photography and Art Studio is hosting Sanderson's low-quality, uninspiring pieces in their next show. Please, save yourself the cost of a ticket and pour yourself a martini at home. This exhibit won't be worth the cab fare."

I sat back and read the last line one more time. "Wow. Scathing hardly works," I muttered.

"What's that, dear?" Nana called from the kitchen. She and Hannah had continued their Sunday morning chat over another cup of coffee.

"Nothing, Nana. Carry on. Just talking to myself." I clicked and typed feverishly. At first, I didn't find much. I managed to reach Kevin's photography website. While I was no expert, I found his photos anything but pedestrian. I knew Cade was equally impressed when he'd browsed through the site. Chaz's opinion piece was not surprising given what I'd witnessed myself. It also sounded like nothing more than sour grapes. I carried on with my search, assuming that the opinion piece meant nothing and carried little weight. I was wrong.

It was only a small entry, a press release from five years earlier. "It is with profound regret that the Metropolitan Photography and Art Studio has cancelled the event— Shadows from Sanderson. Tickets will be refunded promptly." I glanced back to the date of the opinion piece. It was published just a month before the show. Had Chaz caused the show to be cancelled with his incredibly mean article? If so, that would certainly be a good motive for murder. Kevin had to have been devastated by the whole thing. But why now? Had he finally had enough of Chaz's bullying?

While Kevin had made his feelings about Chaz clear, why would he have joined a club with Chaz as the president? Was it part of an elaborate scheme to get within striking distance? Had Kevin seen Chaz standing at the edge of the trail taking in the scenery and decided that was his chance? This new revelation certainly added some spice to it. I'd been focused on the alleged affair, but it seemed Kevin Sanderson had a lot more reason to give Chaz that little nudge over the cliff. I badly wanted to keep this nugget secret, but it would almost be like cheating. I needed to give law enforcement a fair chance. Plus, it was an excuse to text Dalton.

"I found something interesting about the case. We should talk." I closed my laptop and got up for a second cup of coffee. I heard my phone beep with a return text. No need to look to eager.

nineteen

· · ·

DALTON'S RETURN text had mentioned that he was in town, stopping for a coffee and that he could swing by the house. Nana and Hannah had really stretched out their coffee chat. They were each on their third cup, and their words were getting much faster, like those fast talkers at the end of commercials that list all the warnings and disclaimers at supersonic speed so no one has a clue what they're saying but the companies still have a legal leg to stand on. I thought it might be better not to have Dalton stop by the house, what with the two women hyped up on caffeine and always nudging and teasing me about Ranger Braddock. All I needed was two coffee-buzzed octogenarians bringing up my embarrassingly crazy crush on him in school, and I would pack up and leave Ripple Creek for good. Or, at least, possibly until the following Christmas. (Nana made the best cornbread stuffing and gravy for holiday dinners.)

I splashed on a bit of mascara. It wasn't entirely necessary for the investigation but then it wouldn't hurt it either. Dalton's truck was parked in front of the coffee shop. Most of the coffee drinkers had already had their lattes and espressos for the morning. I was glad to see there were only a few people lingering at the tables. Dalton was sitting at a back table, the one that was tucked into a nook where students and couples on dates usually sat to be partially out of view. He glanced up from his phone and waved to me. The butterflies were back, but they were pretty low-key. Then again, it was Sunday morning, where low-key was sort of expected. My mind drifted back to the night before. Had those butterflies been there when I was anticipating a kiss from my dinner host? I couldn't remember feeling them. But that didn't mean anything, I quickly told myself. I was quite disappointed when the kiss didn't come to fruition, so that should mean something. I just didn't know what.

"What can I get you?" Dalton asked. "My treat."

I patted my stomach. "I'm stuffed to the gills with Sunday morning waffles."

Dalton groaned. "Oh man, was it waffle Sunday? I'll be thinking about those waffles all day. Especially after the semi-stale pieces of toast I had this morning. I've been so busy, things inside my refrigerator are starting to take on a life of their own."

I was pleased to hear that he was still living the bachelor life in his cabin off the highway. I was sure he could have a nice place up at the resort with his fiancée if he wanted. Or maybe there really was trouble in paradise. And how would anything having to do with Crystal Miramont be considered paradise? Every once in awhile I allowed myself a catty thought when it came to Dalton's future wife.

I slid onto the upholstered bench that hid me from view from the rest of the shop. Had Dalton planned it that way so people wouldn't see us sitting together? It was probably a silly thought. I was blaming it on consuming far too much maple syrup.

"How is the case going?" I started.

"It's not going anywhere at the moment. I'm going to conduct another set of interviews. Everyone in the club had good reason to dislike the victim. While they've all been putting on a good show of shock about the whole thing, Fiona was the only one who seemed genuinely sad about it. Shayla admitted that she never liked Chaz. He was a bully, always criticizing everything she did. She said her lifelong dream is to become a professional photographer. She works in a sewing machine shop in the city, and she badly wants to get out and stretch her creativity. Those were her words. That's why she joined the photography club. She said as mean and unlikable as Chaz was he knew his trade. She said she'd learned a lot from him despite how he treated her."

I was nodding along. "I witnessed at least two incidents where he harshly lectured her, and always in front of other people. Skilled maybe but hardly a professional, that's for sure. Did they stick to their stories? That everyone was asleep in their tents during the murder?"

"Yes. No one has a solid alibi because they were all in their own tents. Fiona was still asleep when Chaz woke and left

the tent. At least, that's what she told me in the interview."
There was a little doubt in his tone that grabbed my attention.

"Do you think she lied?" I asked.

"I don't know. How does someone keep sleeping when the person next to them crawls out of their sleeping bag, makes the usual noises trying to get dressed, and then unzips the tent flaps?"

"That would certainly wake me," I said. "It's close quarters, so it would be hard to slip out unnoticed. Just the cool air rushing in as the flap opened would make me bolt upright. But didn't Fiona use a sleep aid? I could swear I heard Shayla say that."

"Yes, and that might be why she didn't wake." Dalton looked unhappy as he spun the cup around in his hand a few times before looking over at me. (Heart be still—and you annoying butterflies too, please.) "There's little evidence. No murder weapon for this one. There's still even question on whether or not this was murder."

"The gum wrapper," I blurted. "That's how I found Chaz. A silver wrapper from cinnamon gum was fluttering near the edge of the trail, right where he went over the cliff. An edge of it had gotten stuck under a rock, and it was flopping around in the breeze like a fish." I reached into my pocket and pulled out the wrapper. Dalton was looking more than a little skeptical that a loose wrapper was evidence. "I know this seems trivial since trash can easily break free at a breezy campsite, but it just so happens that Kevin Sanderson chews cinnamon gum."

He took a whiff of the wrapper. "It's faint but it's definitely cinnamon. Still, if he was at the campsite, it makes sense that one of his gum wrappers could have blown off."

"I agree but here's the interesting nugget I uncovered when I was doing research for the case."

He smiled. "The case?"

I shrugged. "Consider me an unofficial partner. Do you want to hear the nugget or not?"

He rested a forearm along the edge of the table. "I'm all ears."

"I found an opinion piece that Chaz Voorman wrote five years ago where he did a harsh, frankly cruel, takedown of Kevin Sanderson's work. Apparently, Kevin was scheduled to show his photographic work at a big art studio, but the event was cancelled. No reason given. I think it was because of the piece Chaz wrote."

Dalton's brows inched up. "That sure sounds like motive, but why now? Why five years later?"

"Maybe the opportunity presented itself, and Kevin decided to go for it."

"Dalton?" a voice that was all too familiar but a little higher pitched than usual stopped the conversation cold.

I couldn't see Crystal because I was still in the nook, but I did have a clear view of Dalton. His expression looked strained. There was certainly no smile for his fiancée. It seemed his whole body was tensed up behind the little table.

I could see Crystal now, but she hadn't turned my direction yet. "Dalton, why didn't you return my texts?" she asked sharply. As she finished the question, her gaze floated my direction momentarily and then her face snapped fully my way. "Scottie." My name came out bitterly. "What are you doing here?" she barked next.

"Scottie had some information about the case I'm working on," Dalton said. He wasn't hurrying or trying to make amends for the two of us sitting together in a coffee shop. He told her plainly, and he even added in a chin lift as if taunting her to argue with him about it. The whole scene was my cue to leave. Unfortunately, I had to awkwardly slip by Crystal. She stood her ground, angrily, arms crossed and with an expression that sent a chill through me. Not that I was worried for myself. I just felt sorry for Dalton. What had he gotten himself into?

I smiled weakly at Dalton. "I hope the information helps."

"Thanks again. I'll keep you posted."

I didn't say goodbye to either because niceties would get lost in the thick tension between them.

"Why on earth would you keep her posted?" It was the last angry question I heard Crystal spit out before I stepped out of the coffee shop. I would have liked to have heard Dalton's explanation, but since my presence seemed to only disrupt *paradise*, I decided it was better if I made a quick exit.

One thing was certain, I did not just leave behind a soon-to-be-wed couple overwhelmed with joy and love. I shouldn't have taken such pleasure in that. I was sure Dalton was hurting. Still, it was hard not to be a little pleased.

twenty

· · ·

THE CAMPERS WERE STILL in town. I had a chance to talk to each suspect before they packed up to head back down the mountain. Dalton mentioned he would be interviewing each one in depth again, but something told me he'd be held up at the coffee shop. I drove quickly over to the trailhead. I realized after I parked that the club van was no longer there. I was sure they were still in town, but it was reasonable to assume someone had gone to town for breakfast or supplies. Speaking of which, Roxi sent a text before I got out of the car.

"Your shortbread was a big hit. What's next?"

I texted back. "Haven't decided yet."

"Everyone loves a good chocolate chip cookie," she replied.

"That's a good idea. We'll plan some for next Saturday." It wasn't exactly the business model I'd been dreaming of, but I was thrilled to be selling baked goods. With any luck, I'd have a fan base by the time the bakery doors opened.

I sighed as I stared out the window at the start of the trail. It wasn't a long or particularly arduous hike up to Blue Jay Ridge, but I was hoping to talk to at least a few of the suspects. It had been a little cold for a bicycle, so my exercise schedule from summer had taken a big hit. And I did eat a large, butter-drenched waffle this morning. A jaunt up the hill was not going to kill me. With any luck, I'd find someone up at the camp.

Another bonus was that the view from parts of the trail was breathtaking in autumn. There were a few people ahead on the trail taking selfies and enjoying the fall scenery. A sea of gold filled the various hills and valleys. The aspen leaves vibrated wildly making the entire landscape come alive. A hawk circled, slowly, methodically over a deep ravine. Its soft, mournful shrieks echoed off the surrounding mountainsides. A nature photographer might have paused with a camera to take a shot of the majestic bird sweeping effortlessly through the air, but I was someone who preferred to enjoy the experience as it was happening. I was spoiled because most of my life had been filled with scenes like the one in front of me. Nature everywhere, all the time. The good, the bad and the ugly. (Rattlesnakes fall into two of those categories. Easy to guess which ones.)

I heard a cough around the next bend and discovered Allen standing on a precipice overlooking the natural pond below. He wasn't wearing a camera. He covered his mouth and coughed again.

"Hope you're not getting sick," I said as I reached him.

He lifted his sunglasses to get a better look at the person addressing him. A polite smile followed. "Hello again. Actually, I think it's the dry air and that constant breeze. I've had a tickle all morning."

"Dryness and constant breezes are unavoidable up here. Sometimes, I wake up and my eyes are so dry, I force myself to yawn just to produce some kind of moisture."

"That would explain why my eyes have been so itchy every morning. I'll be glad when the ranger gives us the okay to leave. I'm not sure why he asked us to stick around. Some sort of bizarre notion that Chaz was pushed." He glanced down at his own feet standing dangerously close to the edge of a cliff. After what had happened to his friend, it seemed he might take more precaution. Instead, he moved his foot forward, causing a mini avalanche of dust and gravel to break away from the edge. "It's easy to get too close. You get carried away at the scenery or find a subject that grabs your focus, next thing you know, the ground beneath your feet gives way and you tumble over the side." It seemed Allen was intent on coming up with a scenario to explain Chaz's death that didn't include murder. Was it because he pushed Chaz?

I might have been playing with fire so close to the edge of a cliff. Especially if Allen was the killer. I stepped back just in case. "But we know Chaz was not taking photos because he didn't have his camera with him."

"Ranger Braddock said his phone was in his pocket.

Smashed to pieces, of course, but it's possible he was taking pictures with his phone."

"Is that normal? For photographers to take photos with their phones when they have so much expensive equipment at their disposal?"

Allen's grin seemed ill-timed given the circumstances. "You can't have your camera with you at all times. I take some of my best shots with my phone. Things happen suddenly, and you don't have time to grab a camera. Especially in nature." He was sticking with his theory of Chaz's death being an accident.

"Wouldn't he have been holding the phone?" I asked.

"Look, I didn't say he was absolutely taking photos. I'm just saying it's easy to get carried away and not watch your step. There are plenty of dangers out here in nature." His mood grew darker. I stepped back again. "You must have been talking to the ranger. You're the one who found Chaz, and even you thought it was an accident. What's that ranger up to? Boy, these small towns sure handle things in weird ways."

"Nothing weird about murder or our small town." The second part might have been a little true, but I only liked to hear it from locals. Out of towners did not get to call our town weird. "Naturally, I thought Chaz had slipped down the mountain when I first spotted him out there on that ledge, but think about it. If you slipped down this edge right now —" I pointed out the obvious. "Would you leap out or just slide down?"

He stared down into the deep crevice below. "I'd slide

down I suppose, but if I hit a rocky ledge I might be hurtled farther out."

"There might be a little bounce, but the human body is not made of rubber. I'm not trying to start trouble. I just want to know what happened. I am somewhat involved because I found Chaz. Basic physics doesn't really line up with where Chaz landed. It seemed there was more impetus behind his death than just an accidental fall."

Instead of continuing a defense of his theory, he nodded reluctantly. "I guess he was out there pretty far. I can't believe anyone in the club would have done this on purpose. I guess I don't want it to be true. These people are my friends."

"That's perfectly understandable. I noticed the van was gone. Are you here alone?"

"They went to get some food. I needed time to reflect. Honestly, I was standing here trying to recreate the whole thing in my mind, to prove to myself that Chaz had fallen accidentally."

I stepped back again to give him more room. "Allen, why don't you come off that ledge now. The last thing your friends need is another tragedy."

He took a deep breath and moved away from the edge. "You're right. That was careless of me. I thought if I could step into Chaz's shoes for a second, I could figure out what happened."

"Let me walk you back to camp." We both turned to head up the path.

"This started as such a nice weekend," Allen said. "I just don't understand." He paused with an idea. "Is it possible

Chaz turned to find a bear or mountain lion heading his direction, and without thinking he jumped, forgetting he was on the edge of a cliff?"

"You know Chaz a lot better than me," I noted. "Did he strike you as the type who would panic and do something reckless because he spotted a wild animal? There was no indication at camp that a bear had walked through. Trust me, they leave bread crumbs, both literally and metaphorically."

Allen's face dropped. "You're right. That was a silly suggestion. Chaz had come face to face with lions, tigers, all kinds of dangerous animals. And he always got the shot. I guess I'm just looking for answers. I hate to think it was someone in the club."

"It's understandable, Allen. You're still in shock as well, so don't be too hard on yourself." The last few minutes had started with me seriously considering that Allen was the killer. He'd acted oddly and was upset, moody. He seemed to be grabbing at any explanation for Chaz's death other than possible murder. Now I had a sense of how much this whole thing had distressed him. While I hadn't checked him off the list entirely, he seemed far more innocent by the time we hiked the rest of the trail.

twenty-one

. . .

ALLEN DIDN'T SEEM to mind that I lingered around the campsite. I helped him pack up some of the cooking utensils. Without good evidence, Dalton probably couldn't ask them to stay in town much longer. Shayla, Fiona and Kevin returned to the campsite about half an hour later. Kevin reached the top of the trail first. He looked solemn and grumpy beneath the shade of his hat brim.

Fiona arrived next. She was carrying a coffee in one hand and an umbrella in the other. She looked far less upset than the day before. It seemed she'd come to grips with the loss and was now processing how she'd move on without Chaz. Or maybe she'd already had plans to move on without him, instead, starting a future with Allen. If that were the case, they certainly weren't making a show of it. Allen and Fiona basically ignored each other as she walked past the kitchen cart and went inside the tent she'd shared with Chaz.

Shayla had taken her time getting to the site. She headed straight to her tent. From the movement inside, it seemed she was packing up her belongings.

Kevin was sitting at the campfire, scrolling through his camera, looking at photos he'd taken. Fiona came back out of the tent and sat away from the others on one of the three picnic tables. She had a book and her coffee as if it was just a nice Sunday to relax. She had recuperated miraculously.

Fiona looked up temporarily from her book. "Does anyone know when we can finally get off this horrid mountaintop? Have we heard from the ranger yet?"

Allen had just finished stacking tin cups and plates into a box. "I got a text that he was coming up here to talk to each of us again."

Fiona grunted in irritation.

Shayla popped her head out of her tent. "Do you think we'll be able to go after that? I was hoping we'd get on the road this afternoon."

Kevin glanced back at Shayla. "There's no telling how this will all play out. The ranger thinks one of us is a killer."

Shayla ducked back into the tent at the word killer.

"You sure are callous about this," Allen said sharply to Kevin. "We all know you disliked Chaz."

Kevin laughed dryly. "Me? I wasn't the one playing footsie with Chaz's girlfriend."

Fiona gasped. "There was no footsie," she countered.

Kevin rolled his eyes. "Please, did you two think you were actually being discreet? Chaz knew too. His big ego just wouldn't allow the idea to take hold."

Allen pointed at Kevin with a spatula. "See, you don't even try to hide your disdain for Chaz."

Kevin looked hard at him. "I wasn't the one waiting to start a future with his girlfriend." He motioned toward Fiona. She wriggled on her bottom, pretending to be shocked by all the innuendo being tossed about. "I even overheard you two plotting to make Chaz look bad by messing with the books. You thought you could get him kicked out of the club altogether."

Allen realized holding various kitchen utensils wasn't helping his point. He slammed down the spatula and moved closer to Kevin. I hoped that photographers weren't the violent type because I hated to have to break up a fist fight. Tempers were definitely flaring. Even the blue jays and sparrows that had been skittering around the campsite searching for dropped morsels had taken off.

"I wasn't the one who had his illustrious photography career destroyed by Chaz Voorman."

Now we were getting to the good stuff. I'd sort of camouflaged my presence by helping out with the packing. No one seemed to mind that I was now privy to the whole airing of the club's dirty laundry.

Kevin's jaw was tight, but he lifted his chin. "I'm glad you consider my career illustrious."

"You know what I mean, and if you were listening, I made reference to the point that the career was destroyed, even before it really got started. That was all due to Chaz's opinion piece in *Photo Monthly*."

I pretended to be busy packing dry goods into a box, but

my ears were practically jumping in the direction of their conversation. I'd been right about the opinion piece. Chaz's article had caused Kevin's photo exhibition to be cancelled. That had to be incredibly devastating.

"My career is doing just fine," Kevin said curtly. "I'm making a nice living off my photos, which is more than you can say for those Polaroid quality still lifes you're snapping with your camera." That comment brought Allen closer to the campfire ring where Kevin was standing his ground, lobbing insults and defending his career. Sizing the two men up, in case I had to step in, it seemed Kevin had the upper hand. He was considerably bigger in size, and something about his rough flannel shirt and faded cargo pants gave him a tougher edge. Allen, on the other hand, was wearing spotless black jeans and a black sweater. His thick blond hair was brushed neatly off his face. Nothing about him said tough guy with an effective right hook.

Allen wasn't backing off. "Let's face it—when they cancelled that exhibit your reputation took a huge hit. Chaz did it on purpose. He hated you as much as you hated him."

Kevin had seemingly reached the end of his tether. He stomped toward Allen fast enough to cause Allen to reach for the first thing. Unfortunately, it was the same worn out, slightly bent spatula. Kevin laughed. "What are you going to do? Flip me over when I'm done?"

"You killed him," Allen finally blurted what he'd been meaning to say all along. "Why don't you just confess, so the rest of us can leave this place for good?"

"I didn't kill Chaz. You did. That's why you're trying to pin it on me. It's the number one playbook for a killer. Blame it on someone else."

Shayla came out of her tent with a dramatic burst and a determined expression. "This is monstrous behavior. Chaz is dead," she said with a shaky voice. "And you two can't even learn to be civil with each other at this terrible time. We're supposed to be in mourning." She wiped her eyes. "You should both be ashamed of yourselves."

"In mourning?" Kevin asked cynically. "Never, for that man." He stomped toward his tent and turned back before slipping inside. "I hated Chaz, but I didn't kill him. That means one of you did." With that touch of drama, he disappeared inside his tent.

Allen looked over at Fiona. She glared back at him and then casually sipped her coffee. If they had been together, it seemed that relationship had ended. It sort of muted the motive for Allen. If he wasn't going to end up with Fiona, regardless, why risk life in prison?

After her outburst, an action that I gathered was out of her usual comfort zone, Shayla grabbed her camera and set out on a walk. Fiona tried to stay out of the fray entirely, not even coming to Allen's defense once. Allen continued with his task, but in a much angrier manner as he shoved utensils and pans into boxes

I'd kept silent the entire time but felt the need to make a comment. "This will all get figured out. No need for everyone to get riled up. Ranger Braddock should be here soon, and once he talks to everyone, I'm sure he'll give you the go ahead to take down the tents and leave town." I didn't know if any of this was true, of course. I'd just decided that the last thing we needed was another casualty. One dead man on a mountainside was more than enough for this amateur detective.

twenty-two

. . .

ALLEN AND KEVIN had gone off in their personal clouds of huffiness. Fiona had disappeared into her tent. She'd muttered something about the elevation and the company giving her a headache. It seemed safe to say that Allen and Fiona were no longer an item, unless they were just pretending so as not to draw suspicion from the others. And suspicion was definitely not in short supply up on Blue Jay Ridge.

I'd decided to take my investigation outside of the small confines of the campsite and, more importantly, outside of earshot of the three remaining suspects. Shayla had not gotten far on the trail. She was in nearly the same location that I'd found Allen standing at an hour earlier. It gave a nice view of the valley below, which was home to one of the nicer, more substantial ponds along the trail. She had her camera lifted. My feet crunched a few fallen leaves. She didn't pull her gaze from the camera, but she lifted one hand telling me to stop.

I froze in place. She had something in her viewfinder that she seemed intent on capturing. A few seconds later, I heard a click. Shayla lowered the camera and released the breath she'd been holding. I realized I'd been holding onto one of my own.

There was only one thing I could think of that would have been worth the wait and the breath holding. "Was it a—" I asked as I approached her.

"A bald eagle," she beamed. "Got him as he swooped down from that tree and dove toward the pond. He didn't catch anything. Now that would have been a prize photo, a silvery fish clutched in his talons."

I stood next to her and gazed out at the scenery.

"I think he's in that tallest pine now. I can't see him," Shayla shared.

"Ranger Braddock mentioned he saw an eagle last time he rode his horse up the trail."

Shayla glanced over at me. "Which one of those handsome men is your boyfriend? The smart talking one who took the photography class or the tall, handsome ranger? I sensed a whole thing happening between the three of you when the ranger came up to check on our camp."

"Oh no, not either," I said quickly. "Just friends with both of them."

"Really? Huh, I'm usually better at reading people. I could have sworn that—" She shook her head. "Never mind. None of my business."

I was relieved she dropped the subject. After this morning's coffee shop debacle, I was worried Dalton would go out of his way to avoid me. For some reason, Crystal took extra offense whenever she caught me talking to Dalton and vice versa. The woman was already wearing his ring. What other assurances did she need?

"I thought I was good at reading people too," I started. It was time to do a little digging, and Shayla had struck me as that sort of peripheral person in the group, the one with little connection to the others. "I was sure Allen and Fiona were a couple. I didn't realize that she'd been with Chaz."

We continued walking. Standing on the ledge wasn't making either of us too comfortable.

"I suppose it doesn't matter now. Fiona and Allen were seeing each other. They thought they were being secretive, but every chance they got they snuck off to be together. I think Chaz knew. He just didn't seem to care. I loathe speaking ill of the dead, but Chaz was mostly interested in Chaz. He was the center of his world. He didn't consider many people worthy of his acquaintance." They were strong words indeed.

We stopped under the shade of a spruce tree. "Forgive me for saying so, but I witnessed Chaz lecturing you. It bordered on bullying."

Shayla laughed lightly as she held her camera close. "Yes, he could be a bully. I'd gotten used to it. I grew up with three older brothers, so I'm pretty good at letting stuff roll off my back. I joined the club to learn more about photography. I kept mostly to myself and worked hard to advance my skills." She sighed. "Looks like I might have to find a new club. I don't think there's much future for this one. Chaz was the main artery of the club. He kept it running, planned events, took care of the books. Without him, the whole thing will fall apart."

"That's a shame," I said. "I was sure one of the other members would step up to the task. I suppose if Chaz was running everything, those are hard shoes to fill."

"I'm just as glad. I'll find another group. To be honest, this one had way too much drama. Lots of fighting and backstabbing. Like you saw at the campsite. I joined to learn skills. Everyone else was here to advance their career. It meant something to be part of Chaz's club. That's why they're all sore at each other. They just lost an important connection to the world of professional photography." For someone who didn't care for all of the drama, she sure understood the politics of the group.

"But what about Kevin?" I asked. "It seems he already has a successful career with no help from Chaz. The opposite, in fact."

Shayla scrunched up her face. "Yes, Chaz wrote a brutal critique of Kevin's work. What Allen said was true. Kevin had a large, important exhibit of his work planned, but Chaz's article caused the studio owners to rethink the whole thing. They cancelled it mere weeks before his work was to go on display. Kevin does well, but his career was on a much bigger track until Chaz sent it off the rails."

A horse's snort pulled our attention down the trail. A small cloud of dust and the rear end of Dalton's horse were all I could see. He'd just turned around the bend. I had about five minutes before he reached where we were standing.

I needed to get straight to the point. "You've been here this whole weekend, Shayla. Who do you think pushed Chaz off the cliff?"

"Well, to be honest, I think the coroner and the ranger are wrong. I had a cousin who slipped and fell off the side of a hill while she stopped to pick a few wildflowers. She survived, but she broke her femur and her collarbone. She was a skilled hiker, but nature is fickle. It gets you when you least expect it. I think they'll find that it was all an accident."

I wasn't about to dive back into physics and body position and all the facts that were pointing toward murder. Shayla seemed convinced, which was probably her way of dealing with the idea that she'd been camping with a killer all weekend.

"But, let's say Chaz was pushed. Who would you suspect the most?"

Shayla rubbed her temple in thought. "Hmm, I don't know. Allen and Kevin seem the obvious choice. Allen liked Fiona, and she was Chaz's girlfriend. Kevin's career lost its trajectory after Chaz's opinion piece. But it seems interesting that we're only focused on the men. The last few times the club has been on an outing, Fiona has argued with Chaz. She was so sick of him before we even reached the campsite, she asked him to sleep out on the benches or under the stars. She didn't want him in their tent." Shayla smiled coyly. "I happened to overhear them during their argument. I was out collecting kindling, and they'd walked to a clearing to discuss it. They didn't know I was standing nearby. I'm sure it's farfetched to think Fiona pushed Chaz off the cliff. Just like it's farfetched to think any one of us did it. But yesterday, I was having to hold Fiona's hand and bring her glasses of water. Today, she's acting as if it never happened. It was a quick recovery."

"I noticed that too." Those were the last words I got in before Kentucky's soft snort blew again. His muzzle came around the bend first. Dalton had seen my car and was not the least bit surprised to see me.

He was wearing his uniform, but he'd pulled on his cowboy hat for the ride up the trail. He pulled down the brim in greeting, like a true western hero. "Miss Ryzen, Miss Ramone."

Dalton stopped Kentucky on the trail. "I'm riding up to talk to everyone. Are you going to be heading back soon?"

"Yes," we both answered at the same time.

Dalton grinned at me from under his hat. "I meant Miss Ryzen. Your presence won't be needed, Miss Ramone." It was hard not to snicker a little at him calling me Miss Ramone.

"Well, Ranger Braddock," I said pointedly. "Last I heard, this was a public trail."

His brow raised in irritation. "Good day, ladies." He pressed his boots into the horse's sides, and with another snort and grunt, Kentucky continued up the trail.

Shayla was staring at me when I turned to her. "Are you sure there's not something between you two?"

I shrugged. "Nope, just friends."

Shayla shook her head. "I must be losing my touch."

twenty-three

. . .

I WAS at a disadvantage to be sure. I stood my ground and
stayed on Blue Jay Ridge on the very solid grounds that it
was a public recreation site. Technically, Dalton could have
pulled some rank and ordered me off because it was also a
crime scene. Instead, he pretended to ignore me and got to
work interviewing everyone. Kentucky stood in a nearby
patch of dried grass and nibbled happily as Dalton began his
interviews. He used the picnic tables off to the side of the
camp to talk to each person individually. I positioned myself
on the campfire bench closest to the picnic tables, hoping I
could do a little investigative eavesdropping. (It was eavesdropping but with an important purpose.) He'd started with
Shayla. I wondered if she'd tell him the same story about her
cousin and how this was just an accident. I quickly discovered, to my dismay, that I couldn't hear the conversations at

the table. However, I could still keep an investigative eye on the interactions at the campsite.

Fiona looked put out by the whole thing as she huffed and puffed around the site looking for a snack. Allen had packed up everything, hoping they'd be able to leave right after the interviews. It seemed he didn't want to waste a second of time getting off the mountain. He'd heard Fiona's quest for a snack and had quickly unpacked some of the food boxes to find a box of wheat crackers.

Allen walked over with the crackers looking contrite about something. Maybe it was because the two seemed to have parted ways or the fact that he, unthinkingly, packed up all the food before they'd been given permission to leave. Maybe he was feeling the weight of guilt knowing he'd pushed Chaz off the cliff.

Fiona stared at the box of crackers with revulsion. I expected her to smack them out of Allen's hand. Instead, she grunted and snatched the box from him. She carried it over to the campfire and sat down with a plunk before ripping into the box. Allen had followed her, rubbing his hands together in angst.

"Fi, could we talk?"

She shoveled a handful of crackers into her mouth to assure him she didn't want to talk. He sat anyway. I was sitting nearby, putting me in an awkward position. I'd found that murder investigations required me to do stuff wholly out of my comfort zone, and, on that thought, I decided to stick around for the possible drama. At this point, I wasn't getting any strong killer vibes from any of them. There were motives to be sure, but it seemed that if someone *was* guilty, they'd have already taken off. It was easy enough to get a bus out of town. Why were they all still here, waiting obediently to talk to the ranger? Maybe it *was* just an accident. In which case, I was wasting a perfectly good Sunday when I could have been at home baking or working on my bakery designs.

I was deep in thought contemplating the future of my Sunday when Fiona's harsh tone snapped me out of my reverie.

"Why are you still here?" She shoved her hand back into the box.

"Me?" I asked. "In case you haven't noticed, this is a public place. I come up here a lot. Especially when the scenery is full of fall colors."

She cast a sly smile toward Dalton, then back to me. "I think you have a thing for the ranger. I see the way you look at him. You're following him around like a lovesick puppy."

"That's not the case at all." She had my hackles up. "I'm the one who found Chaz, and I'm just wondering which of you pushed him off the cliff. I noticed you recovered from your grief rather remarkably." (Granted, not my finest hour as an amateur sleuth, but she asked for it.)

Fiona's laugh was cold. "Do you think I pushed him off the cliff?" she said it loud enough to pull Dalton's attention away from his interview with Shayla. He shot me an admonishing look. I was definitely going to get an earful after this.

"Nobody knows this, but we'd already officially broken

up. We only brought the one tent, so I was stuck with him. But once we got down the hill, we were going to part ways for good. So, you see, I had no reason to kill him. We were already through. As far as I was concerned, he was no longer a part of my life."

"You didn't tell me that." Allen looked stricken. "Why didn't you tell me you broke up?"

Fiona grinned. "Because of that—" she pointed at him. "You were going to start hounding me to get together as a couple, and that's not what I want. I need my independence, my freedom."

Allen looked as if someone had slapped him. Had he decided to kill Chaz so he could make his move with Fiona? And now he was realizing he'd done it for nothing. Fiona was never going to be his. That would sure make you feel like you'd been hit.

Allen stood up, sneered down at Fiona and marched away with his fists tight and his shoulders stiff. Fiona shrugged, seemingly not the least bit bothered that she'd hurt him.

"Miss Ramone," Dalton called from the picnic table. He was wearing a rather stern brow, and darn, if it didn't look good on him. "May I speak to you, please?" Shayla had left the table. She winked at me as she walked past. It seemed she was still on her 'something's going on with you and the ranger' kick.

I got up, pulled sharply on the hem of my sweatshirt and walked over to the table. "Yes, Ranger Braddock?"

Dalton stood up and nodded for me to follow him into the

trees. He stopped a few feet in and spun around. "Scottie, you're undermining my investigation."

"I'm doing no such thing." I stuck my hands on my hips to punctuate my point. "I'm merely here, hanging out, talking to everyone. Like I said, it's a public—"

He held up his hand. "All right, stop with the whole it's a public place nonsense."

I moved my fists from my hips and crossed my arms. "Well, it's true."

"Why did Fiona say you were accusing her of pushing Chaz off the cliff? Seems like you're getting too involved with this case."

I couldn't very well tell him about the whole conversation and the humiliating part, the following the ranger around like a lovesick puppy part. "I didn't accuse her of anything. I merely mentioned to her that she recovered very quickly from her grief." I dropped my arms and scooted closer to make sure we couldn't be heard at the camp. "I mean, did you notice that? Like night and day. One minute, she's in mourning acting as if the love of her life is dead, and the next, she's shoveling in handfuls of crackers like a ravenous teenage boy. Did you know she and Chaz had broken up this weekend?" The flicker in his eyes told me I'd just given him new information.

"She hadn't mentioned that, but I'll be sure to bring it up in my interview." He peered through the trees. "She does seem to have gotten over the death pretty easily."

It seemed I'd softened him up with my information.

Stupidly, my big mouth ruined it. "See, you need me in this investigation."

His stern brow returned, but it wasn't terribly menacing. "I certainly don't. Scottie, you get yourself into these cases, and the next thing I know, you're in danger. Or have you forgotten the incident at the Castillo house this summer?"

"I assure you I haven't forgotten it, but I'm not in any danger. You're here." I pointed out.

"Yes, but I'm doing my job. I can't be watching out to make sure you keep out of trouble."

"I hardly need a babysitter," I insisted, sounding a tad bit like someone who needed a babysitter.

His expression softened. "Why is it so hard to stay mad at you?"

"I don't know, but don't be too hard on yourself. You were giving it your best shot with the stern brow and all that."

He lifted his hat and scratched his head. "What am I going to do with you?"

"Not much to be done, but I will head down the hill now. I think I'm starting to annoy people up here. I'll leave that job solely to you. Do you think you're getting closer?"

"That's official but since I know you're going to keep bothering me about it, I have my sights set on Kevin Sanderson. He had motive."

"You're probably right there."

"Gee thanks, captain."

I shrugged. "You're welcome. Before we emerge from our tree shaped cone of silence, how did the rest of the morning go?" I kept it vague, but he knew exactly what I was asking about.

Dalton adjusted his hat. Cowboy hats were definitely cooler sitting on his head. "It's complicated."

If there was ever a more cryptic and aggravating answer than "it's complicated" I had yet to hear it.

"How is your *friendship* with Rafferty going?" he asked.

I smiled at him. "It's complicated."

twenty-four

. . .

ON THE WAY THROUGH TOWN, I decided to stop in at Roxi's market to plan our next baked good sale. Regina was standing at the checkout counter. The two women were deep in conversation when I walked in. Regina's white hair was clipped back with small silver butterfly barrettes. Regina considered herself Nana's best friend. And while Nana enjoyed hanging out with Regina, she preferred to visit with Roxi. Regina's parents were potters when the original artists' commune started up in the sixties. Regina loved to tell stories about how she balanced on her mom's knee while her mom threw clay on the potter's wheel. Not certain how she could remember something from when she was small enough to sit on a knee, but no one ever questioned it. It was always fun to hear about the days when artists ran the town. It was a little slice of the musical *Hair* from how Nana described it.

"Scottie, you're here." Regina added in a hug. "I feel like I hardly see you. I was going to give Evie a call later and see if she was interested in a walk. I'm closing up shop early. Now that summer's over, there's no reason for me to keep such long hours." She rubbed her right hand. "And as much as I hate to admit that I'm getting old, I think I'm starting to have arthritis."

"You should see a doctor about that," I suggested, forgetting temporarily, that the original locals were more the holistic style people.

"Don't worry. I've got a ginger poultice that I spread on my hands. It works wonders."

"So, we had another death in town?" Roxi was done with the arthritis talk. "Have you heard anything about it?" I was sure Roxi had spoken to Nana. Her few exaggerated blinks meant she wanted me to spill the beans. Only, there weren't many to spill.

"I heard it was someone from that photography club that came to town," Regina said.

"Yes, the club president fell off the side of the steep cliff up at Blue Jay Ridge."

Regina moved closer with a great deal of interest. "Did I tell you I saw two of the men from that club having a loud argument on Friday? They all stopped in the gift shop for a few minutes. Didn't buy anything," she added with a little twist of her mouth. Nothing irritated Regina more than lookie-loos in her shop. "Two of the men stayed behind. They took their conversation behind the postcard stand, apparently thinking I wouldn't be able to hear them behind a wire rack of postcards." She rolled her eyes to show how preposterous she thought that decision was. "They were quite visibly angry with each other." Regina paused, shyly looking up. "The spinning rack of postcards did not block my view either. Faces were red and I even noticed a clenched fist or two."

"Do you know what they were arguing about?" I asked.

"One of the men—he had the nicest head of hair, gold like straw—he told the other man that he was far too bossy and unlikable and that his attitude was going to ruin the reputation of the club."

"Was the other man dressed neatly in new outdoor wear and pressed trousers?" I asked.

"Yes," she said excitedly. "That's him. Do you think they were involved in the murder?"

"The man in the pressed trousers was the victim," I said.

Regina's mouth turned down. "Oh, that's a shame." She pepped up again. "Maybe that's who killed him. The man with the golden hair. They were quite angry at each other."

"You might be right, Regina." I had no idea if she was right, but she seemed to crave the validation that she'd divulged some important information. It certainly wasn't unimportant. It was another example of how Allen and Chaz were not buddies. Maybe there was even more rivalry than just the one for Fiona's affections.

"Look, Roxi, the gears are spinning," Regina teased as she spun her finger in a circle in front my forehead. "She's going to solve another murder."

"Do they know for sure it's murder?" Roxi asked. "One of the women from the club, brown hair and about so high"—Roxi held up her hand to demonstrate—"was in here this morning getting a sandwich. She said the police were making a bigger deal than it was. She insisted that the man accidentally slipped and fell over the cliff."

"Shayla, the *so high* woman, told me the same thing this morning when I was up at the campsite."

Both women leaned in. Only they'd suddenly lost interest in the murder case and another topic had grabbed them.

"Was Ranger Braddock up there too?" Roxi asked with a teasing smile.

"It does fall under his job description to deal with little inconveniences like murder," I reminded her.

Regina had some gossip to add there too. "This morning, my friend, Joan, was at the coffee shop. She said Crystal and Dalton were sitting at the table in the back corner, and they looked angry with each other. Crystal said a few things to Dalton, and he just ignored her and looked uncomfortable. He walked out without her. Naturally, Joan didn't want to stare, but she was sure she saw Crystal take out a tissue and wipe her eyes. Oh," Regina said excitedly, "how is that new friend of yours, the one at the Gramby Estate? Darn it. I forgot his name."

"Cade Rafferty, and he's fine." I was still absorbing what Regina had said about the coffee shop incident. It was easy enough to conclude that their angry conversation happened after I left the shop. Crystal had sure acted adversely to seeing me sitting at the table with Dalton. It was hard to figure out why. The ball was entirely in her court. She had the ring, the wedding date, the beauty, the wealth... I cut short the mental list because it was depressing me. On top of that, I was worn out listening to Regina switch directions.

"I'll probably go with the chocolate chip cookies next weekend. I'll make big, monster-sized ones and add in some peanut butter and oatmeal to give them a little pizzazz."

Roxi looked over at the display cart, now empty of short-bread. "I couldn't believe how fast those little packs of cookies went. I think if you make chocolate chip, always a customer favorite, you'd better make a big batch. Otherwise, I'll be dealing with cranky customers once they sell out."

"You've got it. I'll double the amount I'm planning to make. Which reminds me—"

"Let me guess," Roxi said. "Brown sugar?"

"Nope. Vanilla." I headed over to the baking aisle.

Regina was not great at speaking quietly, but she seemed to think she was. "Do you think it's possible Dalton and Crystal will break up?" She was working on her hushed tone, but it was more like a library voice through a megaphone. "Wouldn't it be lovely to see Scottie and Dalton get together?"

I returned. Roxi knew I'd heard every word. She smiled and shrugged lightly. Regina, on the other hand, snapped her mouth shut as I arrived at the counter, certain she'd just had a secret conversation with Roxi. I decided to ignore the whole thing. The notion of Dalton and me getting together was ridiculous. I'd have to talk to Nana. She was probably the source of the idea. I paid for the vanilla and said goodbye to both women.

As I stepped onto the sidewalk, Esme sent over a text. "I see you through my shop window. I bought too big of a sandwich for lunch. Are you interested in sharing a jumbo cheese, veggie and sprout sandwich with me?"

It occurred to me then that I was indeed hungry. I texted back. "Can't say no to that." After all the wildly entertaining conversations I'd had today, a chat with Esme sounded more than a little refreshing.

twenty-five

. . .

"I'M IN MY VEGETARIAN PHASE," Esme explained as I walked into the bookshop. Her cats, Salem and Earl, were sitting across from her on a bookshelf, licking their mouths as they stared at the sandwich. "That's why the cheese and veggie sandwich. Don't tell Roxi. I was down the mountain picking up some vintage fashion books a woman was selling on Facebook, and I stopped in at my favorite sandwich shop, Rocky Mountain Hoagies." She waved her hand over the sandwich. "As you can see, it's a sandwich of monstrous proportions."

The golden baked roll was at least a foot long with layers of cheese and veggies bursting out both sides. "That is a sandwich to beat all sandwiches. Your secret is safe with me." I nodded my head in the direction of the front window and Roxi's store.

"Like I said, I'm in my vegetarian phase. Roxi rarely

makes sandwiches without meat." She pointed at the empty chair across from her. Esme had set up a few bistro tables, hoping to one day catch the overflow from my bakery.

I pulled out the chair and sat down. She pointed at my half of the sandwich. I picked it up and put it down on the napkin she'd provided. She'd also set out a cold bottle of tea. "It must weigh half a pound," I noted. I licked my thumb. "And it has avocado. You can never go wrong with avocado."

"I agree."

We stopped to enjoy a few bites.

I wiped my mouth. "What do you mean by a vegetarian phase?"

Esme laughed briefly. "I'm ashamed to admit that I'm one of those crazy, internet-lurking-influencer followers, and I get lured in by trends. I've done the whole caveman style eating. I do not recommend it unless you like your bowels tied up like cement."

I crinkled my nose. "Lots of information but note taken."

"I've done the salmon and rice thing where all you eat is salmon and rice."

"I guessed that from the opening title. Salmon and rice for breakfast?" I asked, getting ready with another nose crinkle.

"Yup. Tried to mix it up, you know, by making it into a smoothie but…"

I put up my hand. "Enough said. Otherwise, you'll be eating this entire foot of sandwich on your own."

"You're right." She laughed. "I guess food isn't the best topic during lunch. Anyhow, long story short, I've now veered toward a varied diet that doesn't include meat. So far, it works, as evidenced by the very big, very chock-full of goodies sandwich sitting in front of me."

I happened to glance toward the window just in time to see Dalton drive past in his truck. (Not that I had Dalton Braddock radar, of course.) I was dying to know if he'd learned anything from his interviews. It seemed like the club members were all willing to throw each other under the bus, but no one had any helpful evidence.

I took another bite. "I haven't had a Rocky Mountain hoagie in a long time. I forgot how good they were. I think it's the bread."

Esme nodded in agreement. "It's always about the bread." She tried futilely to press an escaped slice of cucumber back between the layers of cheese, then pushed it into her mouth. "What's going on with that terrible accident up on the mountain? I heard rumors he might have been pushed. As you know, I met the guy. It's sad to say, but I could sort of see it."

"It's true. Chaz was one of those people who seemed to take pride in being unlikable."

Esme sat back with a sigh. "I almost have to rest in between bites. That's a lumberjack's lunch," she added.

"Except, something tells me vegetarian lumberjacks are a rare breed."

Esme laughed. "One of the women from the photography club came in here earlier. She said the rest of the group had bought sandwiches to eat at the park, but she didn't feel like hanging out with them. At least that was what she said. She sat here on the couch and read a book. Earl curled up next to her, which she didn't seem to mind."

I couldn't picture Fiona sitting on a couch with a cat curled up next to her. There was no basis for the conclusion, but the whole scenario fit Shayla better. "Brown hair, medium height?"

"Yes, that's her. She had her camera bag with her. She even asked permission to take pictures of the cats. She seems to think it was all just a tragic accident. She definitely wasn't too broken up about it."

"She's not alone either. Even Chaz's girlfriend recuperated very quickly from the shock and grief."

Esme sat forward. "Do you think the girlfriend pushed him off?"

"I have no idea, but I do think there was foul play."

Esme leaned closer. I was hoping Shayla had mentioned something noteworthy while she sat in the bookshop. But Esme was scrunching closer for another reason. "I hope this doesn't sound ghoulish, but, first and foremost, I'm a businesswoman and while that's not really a great excuse"—she shook her body once—"I ordered five copies of Chaz Voorman's photography book. I figured, now that he's dead, they might become more valuable and people will be looking for copies." She sighed with relief after her confession. "Am I terrible?"

"No, of course not. You're a businesswoman, and everyone knows that once an artist dies their work goes up in value. I think it was a sensible business move."

Esme relaxed back. "Thank goodness. I was worried you'd think less of me."

I picked up the sandwich. "How could I think less of

someone who has given me half of their lumberjack-sized sandwich?"

Surprisingly, or maybe not surprisingly, I was able to easily finish my half of the sandwich. Newly fueled by lunch, I was feeling energetic enough to get back to the investigation. The problem was there was only a limited number of locations for further investigation. The murder had taken place on Blue Jay Ridge, and all the suspects were camping on the very same ridge. At least they were this morning. As I walked out of the bookshop, I sent Dalton a text.

"How is it going? Any arrests?"

I wasn't entirely sure I'd get a return text. Instead, I got a phone call. "I've hit a wall." Dalton sounded disillusioned. "I just don't have enough to make them stay another day. I was hoping someone might break down with guilt, but no luck. Maybe the coroner was wrong. In the meantime, I've been called up to the—" He ended the sentence before finishing, but I knew the missing word.

"The resort," I supplied. "They didn't used to have so many problems up there, other than some rich women fighting over identical Luis Vuitton suitcases or someone's Ferrari getting scratched in the parking lot. Maybe they should hire a ranger just for the resort." I realized as I stupidly rambled on about it, the guy on the other side had gone silent. "I'm sorry. Uncalled for," I added. It was too late.

"And to think I called you for moral support," he said.

"Now I really feel like a heel. You know what? I'm going to make it up to you."

"Please tell me you're going to bake me a tray of brownies and not that you're going to find the killer."

"I could bake the brownies too. Go do your ranger thing up with the snootie snoots, and I'll take care of things down here in ole' Ripple Creek."

"Scottie," he said sternly.

"Bye. I'll have those brownies for you tonight after you make an arrest." I was speaking with supreme confidence, only I had no idea where to start or how to pin the crime on a suspect.

"Stay out of trouble." He hung up with that last reprimand.

"Don't worry, Ranger Braddock," I muttered as I put my phone in my pocket. "I laugh in the face of trouble." A vivid memory of being held at the end of a hunting rifle this summer gave me pause. Then I reminded myself the only thing my current suspects were armed with were cameras.

twenty-six

. . .

I HAD RENEWED ENERGY, not just from the sandwich but from the fact that I basically, in a few more words, told Dalton "I got this." But I didn't have it. In fact, there I was heading back up the same trail to the same camp. The van was still in the lot, which meant the group was still on the ridge. I'd probably arrive to a mostly torn down campsite, but I could work with it.

I was not far up the trail when I ran into Kevin and Fiona. They weren't wearing their packs or even their cameras. "It's you," Kevin said. It wasn't angry, but it wasn't exactly a hello. "Did you see Allen down in the parking lot?" he asked.

"No one was there. But then, I didn't look inside the van."

Fiona turned her face and muttered. "Surprising." It seemed she didn't care for my snooping around and asking questions. Sounded like the reaction of a killer to me. Shayla had mentioned how the men were instant suspects, but the soon-to-be ex-girlfriend was hardly even considered. Though, I wasn't sure that was entirely true. I knew Dalton interviewed everyone.

I ignored Fiona's comment. "I just came from the market in town, and I didn't see him."

"After the ranger left, we went into our tents to start packing up. Fiona came out of hers to ask Allen if he'd seen her camera, but he wasn't in his tent. We haven't seen him since," Kevin said.

Fiona didn't want to stick around. "I'm going to go check the van." She stomped off in her hiking boots, kicking up a little dust with each annoyed step.

"This weekend is getting to all of us, I'm afraid," Kevin said. "Shayla headed up the ridge to see if Allen walked up there to take some pictures. His camera bag is not in the tent."

"Maybe he decided to get a few more photos before you guys packed it up."

Kevin didn't seem too convinced.

"Or do you think it's something else?" I prodded.

He seemed reluctant to talk at first and even glanced down the trail to make sure Fiona was well out of earshot. Kevin wore a serious expression as he turned back to me. "It's a little suspicious. The ranger thinks one of us killed Chaz. Allen had motive. He wanted Fiona to himself. And now Allen is gone."

"But Ranger Braddock has told all of you you're free to go. Why would he feel the need to sneak off?"

Kevin shrugged and straightened his sunglasses. "Just

think it's a little strange, that's all. I'm going to catch up to Fiona."

I continued up the trail. What Kevin said made some sense. But why now? Why didn't Allen take off earlier? Or was it possible he just needed to clear his head and a walk with a few more pictures would help do the trick?

When I reached the camp, most of the supplies had been packed up. But the tents were still standing, sagging and swaying in the afternoon breeze. There was no sign of Allen. Shayla was apparently still looking for him. If Allen was the killer, was she in danger? I needed to figure this out, and sooner rather than later. The urgency of the moment pushed me into doing something I wouldn't normally have done. I glanced around to make sure the coast was clear and slipped inside Chaz and Fiona's tent.

One sleeping bag, a tartan plaid one, had been rolled up, but a second one was still spread out. A small gray pillow sat at the head of it. The bag was splayed partially open. I concluded that it was Chaz's sleeping bag. Either Fiona couldn't bring herself to zip and roll the bag up because it was too upsetting, or she'd decided it wasn't her job to pack Chaz's things. Her things, on the other hand, were mostly packed away in her green backpack. A small pair of light blue sneakers had been tied to the outside of the pack, confirming that the packed things belonged to Fiona. Chaz's various camera bags and several personal items, including a hair-brush, sunblock and travel shaving kit, sat on top of a towel. A handbook on Rocky Mountain trails and wildlife sat next to the towel. Behind it was a personal ledger of sorts. A pen had been shoved down the wire-bound side of it. A label had been affixed to the front of the ledger that read *Nature Quest Photography Club Minutes*.

I turned back to the flap and peered out. There was no sign of any of the campers. I doubted it would lead to anything, but I was out of ideas. I returned to the ledger and picked it up.

It seemed Chaz held a lot of meetings. According to the most recent entries, on Thursday evening there was a meeting with Chaz presiding as president and Fiona as vice president. The topics covered were those you might expect at the beginning of a campout. Safety procedures, assigned jobs and even meals for each day were discussed. It seemed Shayla was in charge of collecting kindling, and Allen was in charge of first aid. Kevin was on communication duty in case something happened and they needed to reach the authorities. As it turned out, something *had* happened. Only I was sure Chaz hadn't expected to be the thing that happened.

Thursday's meeting didn't seem to come with any objections or arguments. At least, according to Chaz. Although, he did strike me as the kind of man who would have just brushed off objections if they didn't fit in with his plans. I turned the page. It was obvious someone had ripped the next page out. The edge was still tucked in the spiral binding. Chaz had already filled in meeting agendas for the last two days of the adventure. Saturday was listed as the day to debrief about the events of the weekend along with a sharing session about particularly good photos they took. In the evening, they were supposed to cook hot dogs and sip wine coolers. Sunday was going to continue with a chat about what they'd learned and the best parts of the trip. A culminating lunch of grilled burgers and potato salad followed. It was sad to see. Chaz had probably spent a good deal of time planning for the trip. He had little celebrations scheduled throughout the weekend. Instead, the whole trip was a disaster.

I flipped back to the missing page. I held the ledger up to grab some of the sliver of light slicing between the tent flaps. On the top of Saturday's page, I could see the imprint of Friday's date. But that was all I could make out. Someone didn't want Friday's meeting to happen or be seen. Which was it? Did the meeting take place? Did something happen at the Friday meeting that set one of the members off? Or did Chaz rip it himself because he decided not to hold it. With how neat and official all of his other entries were, I doubted he'd just haphazardly ripped a page free of the book.

I closed the ledger. Before I could set it down, the flap flew open and sunlight poured inside the tent.

Shayla stood hunched in the opening, her brow firm in anger. "What are you doing in here? You have no right to go searching around Chaz's things."

"I wasn't searching. It's just I saw Kevin on the trail, and he said Allen was missing."

"So, you thought he was hiding amongst Chaz's belongings?" she asked.

"Yes, well, I guess once I checked inside, I thought I'd look around to see if there was something that might lead us to the person who—" I trailed off. Her skeptical brow lifted.

"I can't believe the ranger and—I'm not exactly sure what part you play in all this—but I can't believe this much time is being wasted when it's clear Chaz's death was an accident."

"You sure are certain about that. Even the coroner thought it was a suspicious fall."

"Please, he's just trying to keep himself relevant. An autopsy is hardly required when the cause of death is so obvious."

"Not sure if that's true." I motioned for her to back out of the opening.

I followed her out and glanced around the camp. "Where's Allen?" Since she hadn't brought him and only seemed concerned about a dead man's personal belongings, I assumed she'd found him.

She lifted her shoulders in a shrug. "Couldn't find him. I assume the others found him down at the van."

I glanced over at his tent. "But he hasn't packed up yet. Seems like you'd all be anxious to get down from this mountain."

"We are. Like I said, I'm sure he's down at the van."

Right then, the rest of the group returned to camp. Allen wasn't with them. Fiona had her arms wrapped around herself. She looked close to tears. It seemed she had a dramatic flair for these kinds of situations. The bit only lasted a short time before she relaxed back into her usual character.

"No sign of him?" Shayla called.

Kevin shook his head. "He wasn't at the van."

"He wasn't higher up on the trail either," Shayla said. "I'll bet he wandered off chasing after some interesting animal."

Fiona still cradled herself and marched across the campsite. "This is the worst camping trip ever," she huffed as she disappeared into the tent.

Kevin was slightly winded from the hike. His beard had grown more scraggly over the long weekend. "I guess we should look for him in case he twisted an ankle or something." He glanced at me.

"I can help," I said.

"Thanks. Let's hope we don't get the same ending we had last time," Kevin said grimly.

twenty-seven

· · ·

FIONA COMPLAINED that she couldn't walk another step due to blisters on her heels. She insisted she'd wait at camp, certain Allen would eventually return. For someone I'd seen snuggling and then later *heard* snuggling with Allen, she didn't seem the least bit worried. She might have been right not to be concerned. After all, what were the odds that yet another member of the club was dead? Kevin's suggestion that Allen took off knowing he faced arrest for Chaz's murder sounded much more plausible than Allen wandering off on some uncharted trail. If that was the case, then Dalton had his work cut out for him. It meant Allen could be anywhere, even on a flight to Mexico by now.

Shayla and Kevin each took a section of the trail. We'd all agreed not to veer too far off from the designated path. It was easy to get lost in these mountains, and we didn't need another casualty. We each carried our cell phones and exchanged numbers. Reception was spotty, but if you were patient and persistent you could find a hot spot in the middle of the dead zones.

My feet were also starting to feel blistered as I headed down the part of the trail that ran along a creek. It was a particularly pretty spot to take photos, which was why I thought of it. There'd been enough intermittent thunderstorms throughout late summer to keep the creek moving at a fast clip. The creek had formed naturally and snaked along for at least a third of the trail until it took a fast turn away from the trail and through a dense section of trees. If you followed the creek through the trees you ended up in a clearing that provided majestic views of the surrounding peaks. Another fabulous place for photos. With the creek to guide you, it was easy enough to return to the trail.

My feet tromped down the hill, reminding me with each step that I'd climbed and descended the trail many times this weekend. I was going to soak my feet in Epsom salts when I got home. I didn't have the time or patience to deal with sore feet. I had to admit, this particular murder case had been aggravating and a little less interesting than the others, mostly because it had inconveniently taken place on Blue Jay Ridge. I supposed the death wouldn't have occurred if not for the rugged, steep landscape. Maybe Shayla was right. Maybe this whole thing had been blown out of proportion, and Chaz accidentally fell.

I was annoying myself with thoughts about a wild goose chase when another kind of bird caught my attention. Turkey vultures, truly some of nature's least attractive birds, were circling something about five hundred yards off the trail. They weren't photogenic, but the birds did a great service to nature by clearing away carrion and garbage left behind by humans. Four of them were circling something trying to decide if it was worth the risk and energy to check it out closer.

I stood there and watched the birds for a few seconds until something frightening occurred to me. It seemed they were circling above the forested part of the creek. The tree canopy was probably what was keeping them from investigating whatever they'd found.

I stepped off the trail and with arms out for balance, I glided gently down the steep embankment toward the creek. Walking along the creek took all of my concentration. Jutting rocks and slippery mud could easily cause an ankle twist. After spending this much time outdoors this weekend, the last thing I wanted was to be stuck out here with a sprained ankle.

I was concentrating on my footing and hadn't noticed that I'd entered the forested section until the sun was abruptly turned off, and the temperature dropped a good ten degrees. I rubbed my arms to warm them up as I continued along the creek. The evergreen canopy allowed intermittent pokes of sunlight. I glanced up to search for the turkey vultures. They were still circling overhead.

I'd traveled along the creek as a teenager, but I'd forgotten how dark it got inside the trees. This time I rubbed my arms thinking about all the creatures that might be lurking in the shadows. I was relieved to reach the end of the trees where sunlight poured in once again. The creek meandered along a few more feet before taking a turn farther away from the trail. I stood for a second to marvel at the scenery the clearing provided. Each peak was dotted with fall colors. Soon, they'd be blanketed in white, but for now, they were bursting with autumn energy.

Up ahead, I noticed two of the birds had landed. They walked cautiously toward something in the creek. I didn't relish the idea of racing toward turkey vultures. Not that they were dangerous, but I was out in the middle of the wilderness and they might not take too kindly to the stranger trying to steal their prize.

I went only two steps when I realized it wasn't just a dead deer or rabbit they were eyeing. It was a person. I raced toward them waving my arms. The birds stayed put longer than I expected or wanted. Once I got close enough to confirm that it was Allen in the creek, they took off with an angry beat of their large wings.

Allen was on his side and his face was submerged underwater. His dead eyes stared up through the current. His camera was a few feet away, also in the water, held to a rock by its long strap. Watery blood flowed off the back of his head. I knew full well I was too late, but my instincts and basic human nature told me to pull his face free from the water. It took all my weight and strength, but I was able to free his upper torso. I lowered him gently to the grassy embankment.

I pulled out my phone and wasn't surprised that I had no bars. My heart raced as I realized I'd happened upon yet another murder. Now, there was one more victim and one less suspect. What if it hadn't been anyone from the club? What if some mad person was hiding out in the wilderness waiting to pounce on victims? I pushed down that thought. It was the last thing I needed at the moment while my body pulsed with adrenaline. I moved around in the clearing keeping an eye on my phone and then I got lucky. Two bars. It was better than none. I needed to let the others know, but now there was a one in three chance that I was alerting a killer that I'd located his or her latest victim. It didn't seem ideal to do that considering I was alone and off the trail. I called Dalton.

It went to voicemail. "Hey, Dalton, it's me. I'm out along that creek that runs along part of the Blue Jay trail. There's another body. It's Allen Lennon. Call me back when you get this." I stared at the new numbers I'd just put in my phone. Which person did I think was most likely to be the killer? I was still leaning toward Kevin, but that might have been due to preconceived notions that men were inherently more violent than women. I had to open my mind to the possibility that anyone could have done it.

I stepped carefully along the creek edge to look for evidence. My foot lightly kicked a large rock that was loose and not embedded in the creek or embankment. I stooped down without touching it. I was sure the dark, wet spot on the edge of the rock was blood. A few feet farther down, past the place where I'd found Allen, a water flask was submerged and caught between two rocks. I quickly envisioned a scenario. Allen had crouched down by the creek to fill his flask with water. His attacker came from behind with a rock and hit him in the head. He might have fallen forward unconscious into the water, but it wouldn't explain why his eyes were open. Unless he'd come to only to discover that the killer was holding his face underwater until he drowned. Any scenario was gruesome. We were dealing with a real monster.

"What's going on?" the voice was light and trembling.

I spun in the direction of the trees. Shayla stepped into the clearing, still squinting from the change in light. Her gaze drifted toward the body. "Is that Allen?" she asked, weakly.

"Yes."

Her head rocked back, and she crumpled to the ground in a dead faint. I raced over to her, sat down and put her head on my lap. I patted her cheeks lightly. "Shayla?"

Her lashes fluttered. She stared up at me in confusion. Right then, my phone rang. Thankfully, Shayla must have landed in a hot spot. It was Dalton.

"Got your message," he said, breathlessly. "I'm just getting to my truck. I've called the mountain rescue group. Are you all right?"

"I am but please hurry. We're in the clearing past the forest of trees. Next to the creek. Dalton, things are getting chaotic up here."

twenty-eight

. . .

I NEEDED HELP. Dalton was a good half hour out, and the emergency crews wouldn't be all that far ahead of him. Shayla was sitting in the clearing, shaking her head and intermittently covering her face to stifle a sob. I texted Kevin and Fiona to let them know I'd found Allen, and there was more bad news. I'd given them my approximate location but certainly hadn't expected Kevin to step frantically out from the trees. He was breathing hard as he wiped sweat off his forehead with the back of his hand. It took him only seconds to absorb the enormity of the scene in front of him. His shocked, horrified reaction seemed genuine but then what did I know? I was an amateur sleuth, still wet from pulling a submerged man out of the creek and crouched next to a woman who'd been in a dead faint minutes before.

Kevin strode purposefully toward us. "Shayla? Was she hurt too?" he asked anxiously.

"No, Kevin, I'm fine," Shalya said weakly. "It was just so shocking to see Allen—" She covered her face again.

Kevin walked cautiously toward the dead body in the grass. I realized, too late, that I shouldn't have moved Allen. It seemed cruel to leave his head submerged in the icy cold creek. The coroner would figure out whether he died from a blow to the head or from drowning.

I left Shayla sitting, her arms wrapped around her legs, hugging her knees close to her chest. Kevin didn't dare get too near the body. His mouth was pulled tight as if he was trying to not get sick. So far, everyone was taking the death with what I considered to be the appropriate amount of horror. Did that leave Fiona? She certainly wanted no part in the search. Was that because she knew what had happened to Allen and didn't want to be part of the discovery? She had been dating both men. Maybe bouncing from partner to partner went terribly wrong for her.

"My gosh, what happened here?" Kevin asked.

"It looks as if someone hit him on the back of the head," I explained. "When I found him, his head was submerged in the water."

Kevin nodded as if he understood, but it was all so impossible to grasp. "Is that his camera?" Kevin moved to retrieve the camera.

I placed my hand on his arm. "We need to leave the crime scene untouched. I've already made a mistake by pulling Allen free from the water. I didn't feel right leaving him in the creek."

Kevin nodded in agreement. "How can this be happening?

It's like an endless nightmare. Something tells me if we don't get off this mountain soon, we'll all be dead." Kevin still hadn't regained the color in his face. "Could it be some sort of homicidal maniac lurking in these hills? I just can't believe any of the club members would be capable of not one but two murders." He glanced back toward Shayla. She'd begun rocking lightly back and forth. "Poor Shayla looks ready to fall apart at the seams."

"I wish I could tell you what's happening here," I said. "Ranger Braddock is on his way. He'll be here soon."

The next figure to emerge from the trees was Fiona. She looked as if she'd been dipping into the sleep aids again. Her hair was smashed on one side, and she stumbled a little, apparently still in a stupor. "I got a text." She held up the phone as if that was necessary to prove she'd indeed gotten a text. She pressed her temple like she had a headache, then made an attempt at smoothing down her hair. "What's going on? Did Shayla get hurt?" Fiona hadn't looked past her. Shayla had stopped rocking but was still hugging her knees to her chest.

Kevin moved urgently toward Fiona hoping to keep her from seeing Allen's body, but he didn't move fast enough. Fiona's eyes rounded and she screamed. It was enough to send the hungry turkey vultures, still perched in the tall pines, off to look for another meal.

Kevin reached her before she dropped to her knees. More drama. Noticeably, everyone was more upset about Allen's death than Chaz's. It made sense. The first death launched everyone into a state of shock. They believed it was a terrible accident. A second death was unbelievable, frightening. There was no talk of an accident this time.

I hadn't gotten the feeling that the two women were even the slightest bit close to each other. They were the only two women in the club. Shayla had come to Fiona's aid after Chaz was discovered. Other than that, I'd seen little interaction between them. Even now, Fiona knelt in the grass, a good distance away, looking bewildered and grief stricken. Shayla had released her death grip on her knees. She sat cross armed and legged in the grass turned away from the grisly scene near the creek. Kevin wandered back and forth between the women, looking entirely lost on what to do.

I was relieved when Ranger Braddock stepped out of the trees. Several of the emergency team members were with him carrying a rescue stretcher and a medical bag. Dalton looked breathless as if he'd run from the trail. He looked at the scene in the clearing. His posture softened when he saw me. The ranger and his team walked straight to the body crumpled in the grass by the creek. They got to work, feverishly at first, but the urgency slowed down to a somber pace when they confirmed what the rest of us already knew.

I moved closer to the scene. Dalton walked over to talk to me. "You found him?" he asked.

"Yes, I seem to have a talent for it. And, Ranger Braddock," I said to let him know something official was coming, "I know the protocol at a murder scene—"

"If this is a murder," he added.

I tilted my head at him.

"Yeah, I know, wishful thinking," he said.

"When I found him, Allen's head was submerged in the water. His eyes were open, and he was staring up at me through the rippling current." I shivered as the sight of his dead stare came back to me.

"You moved him?" he asked.

I scrunched up my face. "Kind of?"

"Scottie—"

"In my defense—what if he was still alive? Wouldn't you have pulled his head out of the water?"

Dalton nodded. "That's what I was going to say. If there was a chance that he was still alive, then it made sense you pulled his head above water. But, as I'm sure you know, he's not alive. He has a wound on the back of his head."

"I think I accidentally kicked, but only lightly, the murder weapon. There's a rock near the creek that has blood on it. It's one of the few loose rocks down by the water."

"Ranger Braddock?" a voice called. It was Fiona. She was on her feet and waving him over.

I shrugged to let him know I had no idea what it was about. Dalton headed across to her. Kevin had sat himself down in his own space away from everyone. He'd pulled on sunglasses to block the sun that was dropping down in the sky and pelting the clearing with harsh late afternoon sunlight.

Seconds later, Fiona was talking animatedly to Dalton. I couldn't make out the words, but she continuously shot suspicious glares my direction. It didn't take a genius to know she was making a case against me. I'd been the person to find both men. Not only that, I'd been hanging around the campsite a lot. If the whole situation hadn't been so serious, it would almost have been laughable.

Here I was trying to help solve murders, and I'd somehow managed to land in the spotlight as the killer. It was a good thing I had an in with the ranger. After all, he wasn't going to get a tray of brownies if he hauled the baker in for questioning.

twenty-nine

. . .

THE CORONER HAD ARRIVED. Fiona and Kevin decided to stick around. Fiona said she felt safer being near the ranger since there was obviously a killer amongst them. It was not lost on me that she stared directly my way as she said it. Kevin and Shayla didn't seem to catch on to her insinuation. Kevin decided to stay at the creek and wait to hear the preliminary report from the coroner. He was still holding onto hope that Allen fell and hit his head. Two accidental deaths would be quite the coincidence, but it was possible. The mountain trails had plenty of hidden hazards if a person wasn't careful or watching their step. Taking photos required people to take their eyes off their feet and focus on whatever caught their attention. It seemed entirely implausible to me, but wilder things had happened.

Shayla was still a mess, so I volunteered to walk her up to the campsite. I ignored the accusative glare from Fiona. She even went so far as to tell Shayla to watch her back. I was about to lay into her, but I decided losing my cool wasn't going to help make my case.

Shayla managed the hike back up to camp without too much trouble. "I'm going to finish packing." She looked at me, her eyes puffy and her nose red from crying. "Do you think you could fill my flask with water? I'm parched." She unclipped her water bottle from her belt loop. "There's a gallon jug of it over by the campfire. It's the last of the water." Her forehead crinkled with concern. "Do you think Ranger Braddock will make us stay longer? I so badly want to get home to my comfy apartment and forget this whole weekend."

"I'm sure if he needs the three of you to stay, he'll arrange for some accommodations. I think we can agree all of you need to get off this mountain."

Shayla nodded weakly as she headed toward her small tent. I walked to the firepit and filled the flask with water. Shayla was rolling up clothes to fit neatly in her backpack as I entered the tent. "Anything I can do to help?" I asked.

"No, I don't have that much to pack." She took the flask greedily and drank half of the water.

"Should I refill it?" I asked.

"It's our last water, and the others will need some when they get back to camp." She shook her head as she rolled up a pair of shorts. "Others. I can't believe only three of us will be leaving this horrid place."

"I'm sorry that this weekend has left you with a bad memory of Ripple Creek and Blue Jay Ridge. They are generally nice places to visit, but I'm sure you won't be coming back anytime soon."

"No, I don't think so." She paused what she was doing and sat back on her heels. "I keep thinking about Kevin."

I sat forward with ears perked. "You think he had something to do with this?"

"I'm not sure, but he certainly had a complicated history with both Chaz and Allen."

"I know about Chaz's article that got Kevin's photography show cancelled."

Shayla was shaking her head. "I didn't know them then, but Allen told me Kevin was devastated."

This part of Kevin's history I knew too well, but it was the mention of Allen that had me practically falling forward with anticipation. "But you said Kevin and Allen had history?"

"They certainly did. About two years after that article, the two men decided to get into a business venture together. They were going to start a photography studio in the city. Kevin cashed out some stocks and sank all his savings into securing a lease and buying the necessary equipment. He expected Allen to pay him back for his half of the business with the loan Allen was trying to get. Kevin was sure, between the two of them, they could drum up a lot of business. Then, at the last minute, Allen backed out of the plan. Kevin never got the business off the ground. That was when he started his online store. He does fine with it too, but I think he was really broken after Allen's betrayal."

I was flabbergasted. "Allen left him with all the expenses and a business that was doomed before it even started. That's terrible. Kevin was hurt by both of the victims." A motive for each death, I thought. Was Kevin our man? He'd sure done a convincing job acting distraught when he saw Allen's body.

"Allen could be a good salesman. From what I read in the various online photography groups, Allen was always in and out of costly business ventures. It wasn't the first time he left a potential business partner holding the bag. Kevin knew about some of that, but he decided to take a chance anyhow. Like I said, Allen always had a good sales pitch."

I sat back on my heels too. "My gosh, that's devastating. Why would Kevin join the photography club with Allen?"

Shayla shrugged. "I'm not sure. I think it was sort of that whole keep your friends close and your enemies closer idea. I asked Kevin that once on our last trip. That was, more or less, his vague answer."

"What do you think the real reason might be?"

Shayla glanced around at her half-packed belongings. There were still some personal items like a hairbrush and mirror to pack along with a short stack of books, two novels and a bird handbook. It was the stack of books that snatched my attention. Sticking out from the bottom book was a piece of paper. It had a rough edge as if it had been torn. It was the missing page from Chaz's ledger.

"Honestly, I don't know why Kevin joined the club, but what if he was just looking for the right opportunity—"

Her statement pulled my attention from the sheet of paper. "The right opportunity to kill the people who had wronged him?" I asked, deciding there was no more time to waste on this case. Victims were dropping like flies, and the suspect list was narrowing considerably.

Shayla rolled her lips in as if she didn't want to say it outright. "I just thought with Kevin's insomnia and all, maybe he was up when Chaz left the tent in the morning."

"Kevin has insomnia?" I was sure that never came up before.

"He says it's something he's dealt with for years."

"And then he found himself alone with Allen, the other person who had harmed his career," I said, a little too quickly. Pieces were falling into place now that there was a second victim.

Shayla started rolling clothes again. She was very precise and methodical. "Of course, all of this is speculation. I don't want to get Kevin in trouble. I just thought it was important."

Shayla had certainly come up with a good theory about Kevin joining a group half filled with his enemies just to keep them closer. Still, I badly wanted to get my hands on the piece of paper torn from the ledger. It probably wouldn't help the murder cases, but it might shine more light on the quiet, pulled back member of the group.

"Are you sure I can't help?" I reached toward the books.

"No, actually, I'm feeling a little tired. If you don't mind, I'd like to be alone to rest my eyes."

I shrank back from the book pile with disappointment. "Of course. I'll leave you alone." I left the tent reluctantly. What if the whole case rested on the piece of paper stolen from the ledger? I laughed to myself. It was outlandish to think that. After all, Kevin Sanderson had a major motive for each murder. Maybe that runaway gum wrapper was the first and only clue this case ever needed. Not that it would be possible to convict someone on such flimsy, cinnamon-scented evidence. Major betrayals by two competing photographers would certainly leave someone mentally scarred. Maybe Kevin only planned to kill Chaz on this trip, but the opportunity presented itself when Allen walked off alone.

It seemed I wasn't going to get my chance to grab the ledger paper. Maybe Dalton had more information on the second murder. I certainly had information for him.

thirty

· · ·

TO MY GREAT SURPRISE, a large group of spectators had climbed the trail to find out what was going on at Blue Jay Ridge. I couldn't blame them. This was usually a quiet, mostly empty trail, but twice in one weekend, rescue crews, the local ranger and, most notably, the county coroner had been called to Blue Jay Ridge. It was a beautiful Sunday afternoon with just enough crispness in the air to require a beanie and possibly a scarf but still warm enough to leave behind the cumbersome winter coats. I recognized most of the faces but wasn't about to start filling people in on what was happening. That was something they'd do on their own, mostly through gossip and rumor. One thing was always certain when the coroner arrived—someone had died.

"Ramone," a familiar voice called to me from the sea of heads. Cade stood about half a head taller than anyone else, but with his dark sunglasses and a scarf piled halfway up his chin, I hadn't noticed him. He elbowed his way past a few people. Some of the more brazen spectators had made their way through the forest along the creek. I had no doubt that Ranger Braddock would make them turn back once they reached the clearing.

Cade and I met on the trail just ahead of some of the crowd. He pushed his sunglasses into his thick head of hair. "I was out for a walk, and I noticed a lot of people heading this direction. There was mention of a coroner's van." He couldn't hold back a smile. "Guess I made the right choice to move here. What better inspiration for my thrillers than a town where people are constantly being murdered." He said it loudly enough to gather a few scowls from onlookers. "Oops, guess that little quip didn't go over too well. What's going on? By the way, I'm glad to see you standing here in front of me. I had a terrible thought and then I texted you and there was no response."

"I was probably out of service." I pulled out my phone. "Yep, just got the text." I read it. "God, Ramone, I hope you're not dead. Text me back, would ya?"

I texted back. "I'm alive." His phone beeped.

"Funny girl," he said wryly. "So, who died?" There were enough curious faces watching our conversation that I thought it best we step out of view.

I took his hand and pulled him off the trail to the same tree and location where we'd first caught Fiona and Allen giggling and having fun.

Cade stared up into the branches. "Hey, it's the kissing tree."

I felt my cheeks warm. "And it's out of view of everyone else. People were going to start asking questions, but none of this is mine to tell. They'll have to ask Dalton."

His face hardened as I mentioned the name. "Right. I'm sure the ranger has it all under control." His words dripped with sarcasm.

"I'm sure he does," I said curtly. "He's a very capable ranger."

Cade's brow lifted. "A ranger who allowed two murders on one trail and all in one weekend."

"I don't think allowed is the proper word," I retorted.

"You're right. Forget all that, Ramone. I'm just glad you're okay. Who died? My money is on the girlfriend with the long brown braid and bright green eyes."

It was my turn to lift a brow. "Rather specific," I noted.

"What can I say? I'm an author. I do specifics. Was it her?"

Just as he asked it, Fiona stepped into view. She looked one part miffed and one part embarrassed. "I'm sorry I didn't mean to—" She spun away and then turned just as swiftly back toward us. This time, one of her long pink fingernails came out like a professor's lecture pointer. "You, it's you. How did you know where to find Allen? It seems awfully suspicious that you knew exactly where to find not only Chaz but Allen too."

Cade looked at me with confusion. "Is she insinuating that you killed them?"

I nodded. "I believe so. Fiona, I found Allen because there was a group of turkey vultures circling over that section of creek."

"You see," Cade said to Fiona. His face snapped my direction. "Really?"

"Yes, really. I didn't expect to find him dead, but the birds seemed very anxious about something so I took a chance and followed the creek. Why on earth would I kill two men who I had no history with and who I only interacted with for a short time on Friday morning? What possible motive could I have had?"

Fiona dropped her face into her hands and sobbed. Cade and I exchanged confused looks.

"What's wrong?" I asked.

She wiped clumsily at her eyes. "I know you don't have motive, but you know who does?" I expected her to say Kevin. She pointed at herself. "Me. Yes, I was seeing both of them, and I hadn't really made up my mind on who to stay with. I think they were both waiting for me to decide. That was when I realized that neither of them wanted me passionately enough. Who waits around politely for the woman to decide?"

"Ah, I see. You were hoping for a good old round of fisticuffs," Cade said.

Fiona's mouth grew pouty. "What's that?"

Cade pretended to throw a fist. "You know, a fight."

"Oh, right. It would have been nice. That's why I decided this weekend that I wasn't interested in either of them. But I didn't kill them. I wouldn't throw away my whole life for those two." She seemed to remember then that both men had met untimely deaths. "I mean, of course I'm upset they're dead," she added as an afterthought.

"Of course," Cade said. Fiona didn't seem to catch the sardonic tone.

"I know that ranger is going to arrest me. He asked me all kinds of questions about my relationships with Allen and Chaz. They always think it's the girlfriend or wife, don't they?"

Cade looked at me to answer.

"Not always. Maybe other people had motive too." Shayla knew a great deal about the intertwined history of the men in the club. I wondered if Fiona ever bothered herself with that sort of stuff. "Is there someone, other than me," I added pointedly, "who might have had reason to kill both men?"

Fiona kicked absently at a fallen pine cone. "Everyone, including the ranger, knows about how Chaz ruined Kevin's career with a mean opinion piece." Her eyes rounded. "Maybe Allen saw Kevin push Chaz, and he threatened to tell the police."

"Wouldn't Allen have told the police on the day it happened? Would he have a reason not to tell Ranger Braddock?" Cade snapped his fingers. "Blackmail."

That word only encouraged Fiona's new theory. "You're right. Allen was always having money trouble. It was another reason I didn't think we'd make it work together. I'm high-maintenance." She said it quite proudly. Even added in a chin lift.

Cade was working hard to hold back a smile.

I hated to throw dirt on the blackmail notion, but I already knew of a much bigger motive for Kevin to kill Allen. "Had you ever heard about a business partnership between Kevin and Allen?"

"A business partnership?" Fiona fiddled with the end of her long braid. It had not escaped my notice that Fiona had, once again, rapidly recuperated from her grief and distress. It had also not escaped my notice that she was batting her long lashes at Cade every chance she got. She brushed the end of her braid lightly over her bottom lip as she gazed at him.

"Yes, a business partnership," I interjected curtly to refocus her. At the same time, I was trying to assess Cade's reaction to her obvious flirting. He wasn't completely oblivious, but he didn't seem to be encouraging it either.

Fiona waved her long nails. "I heard something about a photography business they started, but it didn't go anywhere. Like I said—it was one of Allen's biggest faults. He was terrible with money."

"I suppose the old-fashioned protocol of not speaking ill of the dead has died along with mourning clothes and funeral marches," Cade remarked.

Fiona seemed utterly immune to sarcasm.

A text came through as I moved a step or two out from the tree. "Oh, a hot spot." I looked at the screen. It was a text from Dalton. "Where are you at? I've got to do some crowd control. I'm on the trail."

"I'm just a few minutes away. I'll come to you. I want to hear what the coroner said."

"Ah, a long text exchange with the ranger," Cade said. "Probably my cue to head back home. I've got work to do." He sounded kind of jealous.

"I'll fill you in later," I said.

Cade waved without looking back.

"Wow, he seemed angry that you were texting with the ranger." She had no reaction to sarcasm, but when it came to the interactions between men and women, Fiona was right on it. Her face suddenly contorted. "Wait, are you some kind of undercover cop? Forget everything I just said. You can't use it against me. That would be entrappings or something like that."

"The word is entrapment. But I'm not an undercover cop. And you said you didn't kill the men, right?"

"Right."

I was checking Fiona off the list. She didn't seem deeply or emotionally attached enough to anyone. Committing murder took some level of passion or hatred, and she had neither.

"Then you have nothing to worry about, Fiona."

thirty-one

· · ·

"RANGER BRADDOCK, you look like you've had a very long weekend," I said as we met on the trail.

"Seems like I've aged a year since Friday."

Without thinking, I reached up to wipe a smear of dust off his forehead. It had been a reflex, an instinct. There was a smudge, so I wiped it off with my thumb, but the entirely innocent gesture seemed to stir up a whole lot of something. I wasn't exactly sure what, but as I pulled my finger away, I realized Dalton was staring at me. Our gazes locked as I slowly lowered my arm. It seemed, for a moment, that it would take a winch and a pulley to pry them apart. Instead, it was Fiona.

"Ranger Braddock," she added in a slight hip sway as she crossed the trail toward us. "I'm glad I caught you. Ignore everything I was saying about this woman." She looked at me. "Scottie, right?"

"Yes."

She flashed her eyes back at Dalton. Cade was right. They were a remarkable green. "I was just talking to her and that nice man"—she looked at me again, perplexed—"I'm sorry, I didn't catch his name."

My gaze shot fleetingly at Dalton. "Cade," I said quickly hoping he'd miss it. Unfortunately, the name was one syllable, crisp, with definite consonant and vowel sounds.

"Rafferty," Dalton said with distaste. "I suppose he was just being nosy."

"Or maybe he followed the rest of the town up here to see what was going on. After all, we've had two deaths in a row." I hated that I was immediately defensive, but it was Dalton's fault.

"Interesting how you managed to run right into each other," Dalton said.

I waved my arm up and down the trail. "It's one narrow path. One of us would have to be invisible not to see each other."

"I can think of one person I'd like to see vanish," he muttered under his breath, but I heard it loud and clear.

Fiona huffed, seemingly irritated that she was no longer the center of attention. Her pink nails came out again to point. "O.K. I'm not sure what's happening here. Clearly, there's a triangle in the works, but I just wanted to reiterate— yes, I was seeing both men, but I broke it off with both of them because, frankly, neither of them interested me enough. I certainly wasn't in love with either of them, which makes it quite obvious I didn't kill Chaz or Allen. I don't think Scottie did either," she added confidently. "Now, carry on with whatever you two were discussing. I'm going back to my tent. It's getting cold out here, and I have to finish packing."

Dalton and I stood on the trail. It felt as if all the activity around us had disappeared. It was just the two of us in a newly awkward silence. The easiest thing to do was ignore the last few minutes, including the impromptu smudge cleaning.

"What did the coroner have to say?" I asked, as if all was perfectly well.

Dalton paused. It seemed he was trying to decide whether or not to tell me.

"I won't share it with anyone." I decided to use a general term and skip individual names. Especially because one name in particular seemed to flip a switch in Dalton, and I hadn't figured out how to turn it off.

Dalton lifted his hat and raked his fingers through his hair before replacing the hat. "Looks like someone hit him in the head with the rock. He might have been unconscious when he fell into the water. The coroner won't know if it was the blow to the head or drowning that killed him until he does the autopsy."

I glanced back in the direction that Fiona had walked. "Do you think Fiona had anything to do with it?" I asked.

"Not sure. I'm down to three suspects. Kevin still seems the most likely. He said he was out looking for Allen at the top of the trail and wasn't anywhere near the creek."

Movement in the trees let us know the coroner and his team were about to emerge with the body. We stepped off to the side and dropped our heads in silence as they carried the stretcher with the black bag out of the trees and onto the trail. Kevin walked out behind the procession, his head also hung low. He walked with the body down to the coroner's van. He looked properly sad about it. Was he just a really good actor?

"Is it possible there's some maniac out there looking for random people to kill?" I asked.

"That's always the worst-case scenario. If I don't make an arrest soon, I'll have to close off this trail and Blue Jay Ridge until we find the person."

"Well"—I held back a smile—"I have something that might help. After I walked Shayla up to the campsite, she mentioned two interesting things about Kevin. First of all, according to Shayla, Kevin and Allen were supposed to start a business a few years back."

Dalton nodded. "Kevin told me about it. He wanted to get ahead of any accusations. Confessed the whole thing to me. He was left in debt and was really angry at Allen for a long time. Then he realized Allen was so terrible at business, he'd probably dodged a bullet when Allen pulled out of the deal."

I was disappointed that Dalton already knew about the failed partnership. "Did you know that Kevin suffers from insomnia," I added. "Shayla said he's had it for years. I was thinking that—"

"That he might have been up the morning Chaz decided to stand in the wrong place at the wrong time?" Dalton asked.

"Exactly. Remember, that's where I found the gum wrapper."

"Kevin didn't mention he had any trouble with insomnia."

"Maybe because he knew it gave him a reason to be up early in the morning, before the rest of the camp."

Dalton half smiled. "You seem pretty confident that you've got this whole thing figured out."

"Maybe. How about you, Detective Braddock?"

"I think I don't have nearly enough evidence against the man to make any charges stick. As much as you like to come up with your theories and follow the bread crumbs, theories and bread crumbs aren't enough for a conviction."

I didn't even try to hide how hurt I felt about his comment. "Well, I'll just take my clown show elsewhere." I turned to leave, but he took hold of my hand.

Just like moments before, when we froze in time as my finger wiped the smudge from his forehead, the two of us stood stock-still staring down at his fingers wrapped around mine. He dropped his hand, but I could still feel the calloused warmth of his touch.

"I'm sorry, Scottie. I'm tired and frustrated, and now, I've got a second body. And frankly, as much as I tried to keep the notion out of my head, you bringing up the possibility that this is all random and that there's a crazy killer lurking in the mountains solidified that nightmarish possibility."

My anger was replaced with sympathy. "You came up to Ripple Creek to get away from the stress of working in the city, and now, you might be pursuing a homicidal maniac."

"I hadn't thought of it in such stark terms but thanks for that. I'm ready to turn in my badge. Maybe Kentucky and I should take a trip around the country. I could blog about the whole thing. I hear people make money that way."

"And what of your bride-to-be?" I couldn't help myself. The second I asked it, I wanted to take it back. He was already feeling down about the weekend. My question only compounded it.

"Like I said—maybe I should just saddle up Kentucky and take off."

As badly as I wanted to, I didn't dig into it any further.

A call came in on his two-way radio. He stepped off a few feet to answer it. "Ranger Braddock, here. Over."

"We need you down at the coroner's van. There are far too many people standing around. Over."

"On top of everything else, I have to do crowd control. I've asked the three remaining campers"—he shook his head—"I can't believe they're down to three. Anyhow, I asked them to stick around for a bit longer. I might have to get them accommodations up at the resort. I don't have the budget for it, but I'm not going to have them stay up here. If there is a killer in the mountains, and I sure hope that's not the case, then they're not safe. Are you going to walk down with me?"

I smiled shyly up at him. "Thought I might head back up to the camp. There's something I want to check out." In the flurry of activity, I hadn't forgotten about that torn ledger page in Shayla's tent.

"You're something else." He chuckled. "Here are talking about a possible homicidal maniac, and you're thinking of sticking around out here."

"Well, let's not jump to the maniac theory quite yet. I'm still hopeful we'll solve this case—in house—so to speak. I've got a few more things to check out."

He laughed again. "So 'we're' solving this case. Guess I got that wish for a partner after all."

"I guess you did."

thirty-two

. . .

I STOPPED short of the actual campgrounds. Something told me I wouldn't be welcomed with open arms. I'd been a big part of their terrible weekend. I was sure they would be happy to never see me again after this. I had to admit, I was feeling the same way.

I settled myself a few yards off the trail. It gave me a chance to eavesdrop on the camp while remaining out of sight. At first, my efforts were wasted. There were no conversations coming from the camp. I visualized all of them avoiding direct eye contact and avoiding each other. They were the only three left, and there was a good chance one of the three had killed their two club mates. I probably would have avoided contact as well. Only, here I was trying to stay close enough to the trio to find out what they might be discussing in the wake of the murders. Wouldn't it be wild if all three of them had conspired to commit murder? That seemed even less likely than a homicidal maniac hiding in the mountains. None of them seemed to be close acquaintances. Shayla stood out as the least involved of all. Kevin had negative history with both victims. Shayla seemed to be the one person who had joined the club strictly to learn more about photography. Maybe that was why I hadn't considered her too much of a suspect in all this. But now, the torn ledger page kept poking at me. What was on it? Was it something incriminating?

Then there was Fiona. She'd been romantically linked to both men. She'd screamed with great theatrics when she reached the clearing. Not an hour later, she was fine and dandy as if Allen's death had just been an inconvenience in her day. She'd recuperated with the same alacrity after Chaz's death. It was easy to assume the two violent deaths were caused by a man, in particular, a man who had been wronged by both victims. The women were not off the hook. However, Fiona seemed to have little conviction in her soul to pull off the murders, and Shayla didn't seem to have a proper motive.

As I weighed motives and evaluated personalities in my head, an angry voice up the hill pulled me back to my eavesdropping mission. Kevin was speaking in an unusually brusque tone. "That ranger has me in his sights. I don't know which one of you did it, but heck if I'm going to take the fall for this."

"Well, you don't think either of us killed them?" The response came from Fiona. "You had way more reason to kill them than I did."

"Oh really?" he asked harshly. "Except that you were

seeing both men and then you got bored and you decided you didn't want either of them. The quickest way out of the tangled web you wove for yourself was murder."

"Or I could have just moved out of Chaz's house and blocked them both on my phone. Much easier and I wouldn't have to spend the rest of my life in jail."

I found myself nodding along with what she said. It made a lot of sense.

"I'm not sticking around here," Kevin barked. "I'm going to walk down and tell that blasted ranger that I'm out of here. I didn't do anything."

I timed it so that I stepped into Kevin's path 'accidentally' as he marched downhill. His face shot up, startled by my sudden appearance.

"You seem to be everywhere," he grumbled.

"Yes, well, I do live nearby, and since I've been an integral part of this whole thing—"

He seemed to take back some of the gruffness. "Right. I guess we have you to thank for finding not only Chaz but Allen. Maybe you should join a mountain rescue team. You seem to have a knack for finding people."

"This time it was the turkey vultures who found Allen. I was fortunate enough to know that circling turkey vultures meant there was something of interest down below. I walked that way on a whim. I never expected to find your friend in the creek."

I walked with him. He had slowed his determined pace. The walking and movement seemed to help cool his anger. "Allen and I were not friends. We were both interested in photography. We almost went into business together, but, like I told the ranger, in the end I was lucky Allen bailed on me. It would have been an even bigger disaster if we'd gone through with it. Allen and I weren't friends, just professional acquaintances. I had nothing to do with his death. I don't know how long the ranger expects us to stick around—" The mention of the ranger made him take faster steps again. I had to work hard to keep up with his pace.

"Ranger Braddock mentioned making reservations for the three of you at the resort. You certainly can't stay at the campground anymore."

"Not staying there another night. It's not safe. I want to go home. I've got work to do. I can't leave my business unattended for so long. I've got orders to fill, prints to make. I might have to call my lawyer to get this sorted out. Braddock needs to make an arrest or let us go."

"That all makes sense. I'm sure you're anxious to get home to your own bed, especially with your insomnia problem."

He stopped and looked at me. I expected him to ask where I'd found out that personal detail about him. Instead, I got an entirely unexpected response. "I've never experienced insomnia in my life. My head hits the pillow, and I'm out like a rock. I don't wake until the alarm rings." His forehead furrowed. "Who told you I had an insomnia problem?"

The last thing I wanted to do was create more animosity between the remaining *players*. This weekend had already turned into a blood sport. I didn't need to add fuel to the fire. "Oh, I must be wrong then. I thought I heard mention of someone having insomnia."

"That's right." He started walking again. "Fiona takes sleeping pills. She says she can't sleep outside or in a tent without them. She's the one Braddock should be focused on. Not me."

Dalton met us halfway down the trail, and Kevin didn't waste time with his rant.

"Braddock, either charge one of us, or let us go home. We're all in danger right now."

"I agree. I've booked three rooms at the resort up the hill. All expenses paid. One more day, that's all I ask. Mr. Lennon's death has added another layer to this investigation."

"Should I be calling my lawyer?" Kevin asked.

Dalton's brows jumped up and down in surprise. "That's your prerogative, of course."

"It's also my pocketbook. Lawyers cost money," Kevin said. "I didn't kill those two men. That's all I can say on the matter. I feel as if we're being kept here far too long. I have a life to get back to."

Dalton put on his serious, fatherly expression. It was cute. "Your two friends lost their lives. Don't you think you owe it to them to find out who did this?"

The guilt trip didn't work. Kevin was tired and sunburned and, considering the food had been packed up, hungry. "I've told you neither man was my friend. We were strictly professional acquaintances who belonged to the same club."

"But you had personal history with each man and none of it positive. I really must insist that the three of you stay in town at the resort for at least one more day. I haven't even gotten the coroner's report on Mr. Lennon yet. I was just heading back up to talk to each of you."

"You already have," he insisted.

"Not thoroughly, not about this last death. I haven't had a chance to interview Miss Ryzen at all. If you want to stay down here and rest, that's fine. I'm going to go up to the camp and talk to the women."

"They'll probably just throw me under the bus," Kevin remarked.

"That seems to be happening a lot with all three of you. Once I'm done talking to the women, and once all of you have your belongings packed up, I'll drive you all to the resort where you can shower and rest."

The mention of a shower and rest seemed to placate him. "All right. But let's make this fast. I want off this blasted trail."

thirty-three

$\cdots$

I MADE the choice to linger behind on the trail and allow Dalton to start the interviews without me hanging out in the background. On my way up to the top (my feet were going to need a long hot soak after this) I spotted Shayla off the trail taking close-up photos of some of the last few arctic genetian, wildflowers, soft and white with a daylily shape, that continued to bloom in fall. She was so absorbed with her photo shoot, she didn't notice me pass by. It seemed odd that she was out and very much alone on a trail where two of her acquaintances were murdered, but in retrospect, Shayla was what Nana would refer to as a 'quirky little mushroom'. I had a friend named Annabelle in grammar school who insisted on carrying a briefcase. She dressed like a businesswoman with cute little suits. Nana loved to talk to Annabelle because she was extremely intelligent. I remembered the words genius and prodigy being thrown around even if, at the time, I didn't really know what they meant. (Hence, making the case that I *wasn't* a genius.) Whenever Annabelle left, after a play date, where we almost always had to create some kind of business or shop, Nana would always smile admiringly and say that girl is a "quirky little mushroom." That was Shayla. She didn't fit in with the rest of the group. Was that it? Did Shayla know she was the oddball out? Chaz had certainly let her know every time she was doing something wrong. Was that a good motive for murder?

I reached the camp. The slightest sliver of jealousy shot through me when I spotted Dalton at the picnic tables with Fiona. She was leaning over with a smile that could melt even the coldest man's heart. A light giggle rolled across the camp-site, an odd reaction considering Fiona was being questioned about possible murder. It wasn't the first time I'd heard her giggle flirtatiously. She was somewhat of an expert at it. It was hard to deny that Fiona had all the attributes that were attractive to men. Even Cade had made a point of mentioning her green eyes. However, Dalton sat with straight posture and rigid shoulders as he asked her questions.

After I shook off the ridiculous bout of jealousy (especially considering Dalton wasn't mine to be jealous of) I realized I was alone in the campsite. The picnic benches had been set far enough away from the tent area that I could move easily about without being noticed.

My heart raced at hummingbird speed as a new plan hatched. I glanced back toward the trail. There was no sign of

Shayla. I ducked down in case Dalton happened to move his head the right way or finally take his eyes off his attractive murder suspect. I didn't want him to see me moving stealthily and with the shoulders of a guilty person across the camp.

Shayla had zipped up her tent. I carefully unzipped it and stepped between the open flaps. I was in luck. The short stack of books hadn't been packed away yet. I crouched down and was immediately flattened with disappointment. The piece of paper was gone. To be sure, I lifted the stack of books. No torn ledger page. Just three printed photos. Considering Shayla's and the whole club's goal was to take beautiful pictures of nature, I was surprised to find that not one but all three photos were of Allen Lennon. In one photo, he seemed to be talking and laughing with someone. He had a gracious smile, and the photo really captured that. I was no expert, but it seemed the picture had been taken without him realizing it. It was an unrehearsed, natural image. The second photo was of Allen standing on the edge of a trail (not Blue Jay Ridge, possibly not even in the Rockies due to the variety of trees). He was taking a photo of his own while this one was snapped. Sunlight poured down from the blue sky above at just the right angle that gave Allen a sort of majestic, God-like look. It was a flattering photo. The third one was a little less mythical. Allen was wearing reading glasses and sitting against a tree as he read a book. They were three very nice memories caught on camera. Had Shayla taken them out as a tribute to Allen? Why did she happen to have those three photos with her on this camping trip? As I shuffled through the photos once more, something occurred to me. These weren't random photos. Shayla had taken these through her own lens... and through her own heart. Shayla was in love with Allen. I was basing that conclusion solely on the photos, but I knew I was right.

Certainly, Shayla couldn't be the killer. Why would she kill the man she was so clearly in love with? Unless he didn't return her feelings. I hadn't noticed any interaction this weekend that would have led me to the conclusion that Allen had any intimate feelings for Shayla. He'd been with Fiona for the first part of the trip. Had that made Shayla jealous?

I contemplated taking the photos to Dalton but then it would be far too obvious that I'd been searching her tent. Something I had no right to do. I stuck them back under the book, poked my head out and looked around. Still no sign of Shayla or Kevin... or Dalton and Fiona. The picnic table was empty. As my head poked around like a turtle just emerging from its shell, a tall shadow fell over me.

"What are you up to?" Dalton asked dryly.

I shot out of the tent as if being ejected from an airplane. I landed on my knees and sat back to my bottom. "Uh, I couldn't deal with the sun anymore. Needed a reprieve." My face felt hot as asphalt on a midsummer day.

Dalton had his arms crossed, and he was wearing that cocky half smile that I found so appealing. However, with crossed arms and furrowed brow it wasn't quite as adorable. "An easy solution would have been for you to just go home."

He offered me a hand. I swished my hands back and forth to remove the dust and grit and placed my newly cleaned hand in his. Dalton pulled me to my feet hard enough that I did a small hop forward, landing my free hand against his chest. We stood there, toe to toe, gazes smacked together for a second. I pulled my hand off his chest as if it had been molten hot.

"Sorry, I wasn't ready for all that strength," I said teasingly. "Have you been working out? I noticed your arms looked bigger and—"

"Enough, Scottie. Please. You're going to ruin the integrity of my investigation."

"Speaking of investigations," I said, ignoring his reprimand entirely. I looked around. No sign of Shayla, but I lowered my voice. "My woman's intuition and some very personal photos inside that tent tell me that Shayla was in love with Allen."

His expression flickered just enough to assure me I'd caught his interest. That gave me the juice I needed to continue, unabated and without thinking... unfortunately.

"The last time I was in Shayla's tent—invited I might add —there was a torn piece of paper under the books where I just now spotted the photos of Allen. I was in Chaz's tent—"

"Invited?" he asked pointedly.

"Not technically, no."

"Pretty sure there's no technicality involved. Either you were or you weren't."

"Do you want to hear what I have to say because, frankly,

I don't hear the clanking of handcuffs or the sound of someone being read their rights."

He stared at me, annoyed.

"Sorry. That was mean. It's the sun." I pointed to the sky in case he needed a visual.

"Again, you could be at your house right now. It has a roof and all that."

"Dalton, please. Just listen. I'm starting to get some solid theories here."

He'd uncrossed his arms earlier but for some reason decided the conversation needed them crossed again. "Go on."

"Chaz kept a ledger with club meeting minutes. I browsed through it"—I put up my hand—"And no I was not invited, Mr. Right and Proper. I noticed that the page from Friday's minutes had been ripped free of the ledger. I later spotted it in Shayla's tent. Only, she was inside the tent, so I couldn't get a hold of it. Now it's gone. I think there's something on that page that upset Shayla. Possibly even enough to make her kill someone."

My big ta-da moment was ruined by Kevin's return to camp. He looked about as worn out and bedraggled as a camper could look.

"I need to talk to Mr. Sanderson. Then we're shutting this camp down, and I'm taking everyone to the resort." He looked around. "Where is Miss Ryzen now?"

"I saw her taking pictures out on the trail earlier. Funny, don't you think? She doesn't seem the least bit worried that two people have died."

"Have to agree with you there. Sanderson is still my main suspect. In the meantime, why don't you go home."

"Heading down the hill right now." That was the truth. I'd had enough of the great outdoors for one weekend. Of course, if I happened to run into Shayla on the way, there was nothing stopping me from a friendly chitchat.

thirty-four

. . .

I WALKED DOWN SLOWLY, partly because my feet were sore and starting to sprout blisters and partly because I wasn't exactly sure where Shayla had ended up. I listened for footsteps, breathing, a sneeze, even, but she seemed to have vanished. Adrenaline shot through me. Not another missing camper. Not another grim discovery. Then we really would have to consider the homicidal maniac theory. That thought made me shiver. I was also starting to get cold. The sun was dropping in the sky. Soon the higher peaks would block it altogether, and even if the clocks didn't confirm it, the trail would be bathed in shadows that looked a lot like night.

I peered up to the sky just in case a flock of turkey vultures wanted to let me know something else had happened. There was no sign of them. One thing about being in the mountains and surrounded by a lot of tall peaks—

sound carried and ricocheted and echoed. I was walking gently down the trail, trying not to alert anyone to my presence in case there really was a psycho killer on the loose. That was when I heard a light sound that was distinctive and familiar enough to recognize. Especially because it was inconsistent with the usual sounds of nature. It was paper ripping. I was sure of it, and it was coming from somewhere off the trail. I stopped and realized I was back where the day had started, at the turnoff to the creek. The creek where I'd found Allen half submerged in the icy water.

I paused for a second. What if it was the killer returning to the scene of the crime? Why would a homicidal maniac be tearing up a piece of paper? Did he have a list of names? Had he checked them all off? I doubted that would be the case. It was hard to picture some maniacal killer sitting down to neatly write out a checklist. Another thought struck me that coaxed me off the trail. What if Shayla was in trouble? Death by paper cuts, I mused to lighten the mood for myself. I was feeling more than a little scared.

The waning sunlight coupled with the heavy canopy of trees shrouded the creek trail in absolute darkness. I picked up my pace, turning my head side to side as if I was watching a warp-speed tennis match. I released the breath I'd been holding when I finally reached the place where the trees grew thin and sunlight could once again make the world right.

It took a second for my eyes to adjust, but I quickly confirmed that the figure I saw standing by the creek, in almost the exact place where I'd found Allen, was Shayla

Ryzen. She hadn't noticed me step into the clearing. She seemed to be intently watching something in the creek. I headed toward the water and spotted pieces of white paper floating with the current. She'd shredded the ledger page and sent it down the creek. But why? Was it some sort of tribute to Allen? She wasn't wearing a mournful expression, but she certainly looked shocked when she saw me.

I stared at her for a second, trying hard to read her thoughts. I pieced together everything I knew about the group and that helped me come up with a solid theory.

"That's evidence, isn't it?" I asked.

She pressed on a fake smile. "What do you mean evidence? It was just a piece of paper I found in my pocket, so I tore it up and tossed it in the water."

"Seems a little hypocritical for someone who is supposed to be a nature lover to throw litter into a pristine creek. But then, you threw a human being in there, so I guess the paper was an easy choice. What was on that ledger page?"

Shalya positioned her camera bag on her shoulder and lifted her chin. "I have no idea what you're talking about. It was just a scrap of paper. And since paper comes from trees, I didn't consider it littering."

"Well, I think there might be a few forever chemicals along with the tree pulp, but sure, if that's what you say."

Shayla stomped back toward the trees. "You're a very nosy person. Has anyone ever told you that?"

"I might have heard that before," I said. "But you aren't a great photographer, at least when it comes to nature, and that's why Chaz was so short with you. He'd given up trying to help you. That's why you killed him. It's a shame because I've seen your other work—"

She stopped mid march, spun around and stomped toward me. I shuffled back a few steps. I was close enough to the creek that I could feel the spray of water behind me.

"What other work? Were you snooping in my tent?" she shrieked.

"I was looking for you and spotted the photos of Allen under the books. That is where your talent is, taking portraits of people. Too bad you won't get much chance to practice the skill in jail."

Her face turned to smooth white stone. "You had no right to look at those. And don't lie to me because I know those were hidden under the books."

"Yes, right below the page from Chaz's ledger. I saw it there when I was helping you earlier. It was missing from the ledger. The meeting minutes from Friday, the day before Chaz was pushed off the cliff. Did they vote you out?" I asked.

Her lip quivered vulnerably, but the rest of her expression was pure rage. "They had no right to judge. I was learning. My work was getting better. Kevin was the only person to vote nay. Fiona joined with her two lovers." She rolled her eyes. "That dimwit, with her sparkly, tight clothes and her big white smile. No one ever mentioned that she was a talentless hack. This was going to be my last trip with the club, so I decided to make it the last trip for the club altogether."

"I'll bet it was especially hard when the man you loved voted you out," I said.

Not just her lip but her whole chin quivered. "I wasted my time thinking about Allen. He turned out to be just as bad as the rest of them, arrogant, mean, not worthy of respect. I'd been following him. I always followed him," she admitted unabashedly. "Allen came here to this creek. He stooped down to fill his flask with water, and I hit him over the head with a rock. He fell face first into the water. I thought he was dead, then I saw bubbles. He struggled to turn around, but I held him down until the bubbles disappeared." She said it casually as if she was just mentioning that eggs were on sale at the store.

"You murdered two people over a club membership." I hoped saying it plainly would cause her some regret, some remorse, but it didn't seem to faze her.

"They had it coming." The soft-spoken, fade-in-the-background Shayla Ryzen had morphed into something frightening.

Ignorantly, I pictured myself walking my suspect up the hill to the ranger, so she could make her confession and this whole weekend could be wrapped up in a nice little bow. I'd go home, take a hot bath, soak my feet and sit down to one of Nana's soups, preferably broccoli because she always added in cheddar cheese. But I'd misjudged the whole thing. I still had a lot to learn about facing down killers. Shayla's expression assured me there would be no nice walk up the hill. It dawned on me, rather suddenly, I was in danger. My fight or flight instinct was leaning toward flight.

I turned and took off but didn't get four steps before I was pushed hard from behind. Shayla's hands jammed into my ribs. I took a few clumsy steps forward. Before I could catch myself, my right foot caught on a jutting rock. My knees slammed the ground and my hands followed. I managed to keep my face from hitting dirt. Before I could sit up, a shadow dropped over me and something went around my neck. It was the strap from Shayla's camera bag.

thirty-five

. . .

I WAS in a fight for my life... literally. It took me a few seconds of terror to realize that the mad woman, who'd blithely killed two acquaintances, was about to claim her third victim. She had no preferred method for murder. No cliffs or creeks this time. All she needed was the leather strap on her camera bag. The camera itself kept smacking me between the shoulder blades. I grasped the strap and tried to lean away from her. It only tightened the strap more around my neck. The leather edges dug into my fingers and my skin. I was only able to snatch the tiniest, most meaningless sips of air. The lack of oxygen was zapping my strength. I kept hold of the strap, but she pulled harder.

"I'm not spending the rest of my life in jail because of a nosy woman like you," Shayla sneered into my ear.

Even the tiny sips of air had been cut off. The voice in my head told me I was losing the battle. No. I refused. I let go of the strap and reached blindly around for a rock. My knuckles smacked painfully into one. I tried desperately to pull it free, but it was wedged in deep. Tiny dots started to appear in my eyes, and I felt woozy. I reached around again and found a potato sized rock. It was loose. I grabbed it and swung it back toward my attacker. A thud and a scream of pain followed. The strap loosened. I fell over coughing and gasping for air. Somewhere in the nightmarish chaos I heard a shout.

I sucked in more of the frigid late afternoon air and lifted my face. Dalton was racing toward me wearing a look of horror. He had his weapon drawn. "Stay down, Scottie!" he yelled as he neared us. "Stop where you are!" he commanded.

I'd finally gotten enough air in my lungs to saturate my brain with oxygen. The spots were gone and the dizziness disappeared. I looked hesitantly behind me. Shayla dropped to her knees. Her face fell into her hands, and her body shook with sobs. I could have almost felt sorry for the woman, but as I swallowed, the tenderness in my neck reminded me that I'd almost died.

The next hour moved so fast I'd still only just recovered from my ordeal by the time the county sheriff had arrived to make the official arrest. I was questioned by a woman officer. She took down everything Shayla had told me and what had transpired when she attacked me. It seemed I'd gotten myself deep into this one. Deeper than I should have.

Dalton was finishing up with his official duties, but he kept looking my direction. Sometimes, there would be a look of concern on his face, and other times, he looked angry. I was gearing up for a full-blown lecture. I deserved it.

When he finally finished his work, he headed over to the patch of ground I'd found for myself, a viewing place out of the way of the activity but close enough for me to watch what was happening. I realized then I wasn't ready to hear angry words from him. I'd been through an ordeal, and I was sure a terse lecture would cause me to fall into a million pieces. What I needed right then was kindness. And that was what I got.

Without saying a word, he lowered his hand for me to take. He helped me to my feet. I stared into his magnetic gaze for a few seconds. His finger reached up and lightly touched the red mark on my neck. "Could have lost you, Scottie." His voice was a little raspy.

"I hit her with a rock," I said, not knowing how else to respond. He was right. I'd been a short time away from death.

Dalton nodded. "You got her good too. Smart thinking saved your life."

"I guess it was the opposite—the dumb thinking—that nearly killed me." My voice broke. Dalton took me into his arms, and I let the tears flow. I'd needed that cry after all.

thirty-six

. . .

DALTON HAD DRIVEN me home after everything had been settled. Kevin and Fiona drove out of town so fast there were practically flames shooting out of the van. Something told me it would be a long time before either of them went camping or, for that matter, joined a club again. Dalton had to get back to his office to write up a report. I felt bad that his long weekend still hadn't ended. I told him I owed him some brownies but that I just wasn't up to putting on a baker's hat this evening. He understood. I also had to make him promise not to tell Nana how the day ended. It would distress her to no end. I would have to use some concealer to hide the marks on my neck.

I left out a great deal of the events that took place on Blue Jay Ridge when I recounted the tale to Nana over a bowl of her broccoli soup. (Yes, there was cheddar cheese.) I gave her an abbreviated version.

"How awful that the poor woman thought she needed to resort to such drastic measures after merely being kicked out of a photography club." Nana stood to clear the dishes.

"I'll clean up, Nana."

"Nonsense. You've had a long day. I have a surprise in the refrigerator. I made homemade chocolate pudding."

"And that is why you're the best Nana in the world." She had no idea how badly I needed this cozy home dinner tonight. I carried my bowl to the sink, gave her a quick hug and then dove, like a kid, into the refrigerator for my bowl of pudding. I carried my chocolaty treat out to the front room. Before I could flop on the couch and scoop into the pudding there was a knock on the door. I was still a little on edge, and the unexpected knock startled me. I glanced out the window. Dalton's truck was parked in front of the house.

I opened the door. He'd showered and changed into a pair of black jeans and a green sweater. The butterflies had been exhausted from seeing him all weekend, but they managed a nice little dance recital to remind me just how much I still liked the man.

"I came by to see how you were doing."

I glanced toward the kitchen. Nana was making enough noise with the dishes and pots that she hadn't heard the knock. "I'm fine." I held up the bowl. "I have homemade chocolate pudding, so I'm extra fine. Would you like some?"

"After this weekend? Do you even have to ask?" His smile had returned for the first time all afternoon. It was always good to see.

I motioned for him to come inside, and I went to the kitchen for some pudding and a spoon.

Nana looked over her shoulder and laughed. "Already on round two?"

"Dalton is here."

"Oh, I see." Nana curled in her lips and returned to her task.

I carried the pudding out to Dalton and sat next to him on the couch.

We hadn't talked about the case on the way home, and I had some questions. "Dalton, how did you know to come looking for Shayla? What made you think she did it?"

"I'd been waiting for some information on her. Her name didn't come up when I did a search. I traced the name to another name, Carla Vanguard. That's Shayla's real name. And Carla Vanguard had a history. Not a good history. Ten years ago, a roommate of hers was found dead in their shared apartment. There was never enough evidence to arrest Carla. The killer was never found. The information came through while I was at the camp talking to Kevin. And I thought— where did Shayla go? And then I thought, I'll bet my friend, Scottie Ramone, didn't head home like I asked her to. I raced down the trail. It was Shayla's scream that pulled me in the direction of the creek."

"Thank goodness for that rock," I said. "I'm going to be much more wary and respectful of those stones whenever I hike somewhere."

We ate our pudding in silence for a few seconds. The rich

scent of cocoa and the peace of mind that the ordeal was over surrounded us.

"How come you didn't lecture me?" I asked.

"That'll come later, after I recover from the shock that I almost lost you."

His words tugged at my heart. I had no idea why I did it, but I figured I'd earned it. I rested my head against his shoulder.

Scottie Ramone Cozy Mystery #3

about the author

London Lovett is author of the Port Danby, Starfire, Firefly Junction, Scottie Ramone and Frostfall Island Cozy Mystery series. She loves getting caught up in a good mystery and baking delicious, new treats!

Learn more at:
www.londonlovett.com

Printed in Great Britain
by Amazon

26883915R00131